"FORWARD [...] CALLED SPOCK.

"Starboard shields buckling," the Vulcan continued. "Port shields can sustain only two more hits."

"Captain, how about the Turnoga defense!" Chekov suddenly shouted. "In a situation like this—"

"Not now, Mr. Chekov!" snapped Kirk.

"But sir—"

"Ensign," said Kirk, "I don't have time to turn the bridge into an Academy lecture hall. Bring us around to 419 mark 6. Drop forward shields; prepare for warp speed."

"What?" Chekov exclaimed. "Captain, even minimal warp will kick us right out of the system! And with no shields, we'll be defenseless."

"Ensign, you're relieved," said Kirk sharply. "Palmer, take over. Mr. Chekov, get the hell off the bridge. You're confined to quarters."

Look for STAR TREK Fiction from Pocket Books

Star Trek: The Original Series

Star Trek: The Next Generation

STAR TREK®

THE DISINHERITED

PETER DAVID,
MICHAEL JAN FRIEDMAN
AND ROBERT GREENBERGER

POCKET BOOKS
New York   London   Toronto   Sydney   Tokyo   Singapore

An *Original* Publication of POCKET BOOKS

POCKET BOOKS, a division of Simon & Schuster Inc.
1230 Avenue of the Americas, New York, NY 10020

ISBN: 0-671-77958-3

First Pocket Books printing May 1992

10 9 8 7 6 5 4 3 2 1

THE DISINHERITED

Chapter One

"TODAY IS THE LAST DAY of the rest of your life."

Jak Eisman grinned lopsidedly at the man who had just spoken. He stabbed a finger at him and said, "You, Delacort, are jealous."

Delacort took a step back, miming having been shot in the heart. Delacort was several decades Jak's senior, but that didn't stop him from engaging in behavior that belied his years. He shook his white-maned head and gravely placed a hand on Jak's shoulder. "I worked with you, trained you," he intoned. "Tried to instill all the good values that have so guided me through my life. And what happens? You're going to go and get married anyway."

Jak shook his head and tapped the computer screen in front of Delacort. "Don't you think," he observed, "that maybe you'd better get to work? There's a full schedule packed for today." Jak's blue eyes snapped in amusement. His long red hair was tied back in a ponytail that he had only recently started sporting; it had garnered quite a few comments from the other members of the Gamma Xaridian colony research team, but he had ignored them all. Because the only thing that mattered was that L'rita liked it. She had told him that, combined with his rather large jaw, it made him look quite heroic, very much the swash-buckler. He liked the sound of that. Jak Eisman, swashbuckling aide to the administrative head of the Gamma Xaridian colony. It had a bit of zip to it.

Delacort, with a sigh like a stray zephyr, plopped down behind his desk. His office was not only the largest in the building, it was the largest on the planet. The glorious Gamma Xaridian sun was just coming up over the horizon, its rays cutting through the window and illuminating the vast variety of glass and crystal knickknacks that Delacort had been so fond of collecting. They lined many of his shelves, and the early mornings in Delacort's office were usually very impressive. Rainbows glimmered off all of the white reflective surfaces. While Jak detested having to rise so early to meet his duties as Delacort's right-hand man, there was some aesthetic value to it.

Delacort scanned his duties for that day. "The same as yesterday," he said gravely. "And the same as the day before that—debates, discussions. I swear to Kolker, we have—what is it?—seven committee meetings scheduled for today?"

"Eight," Jak corrected.

"Eight. How many scientific committees does this colony support, anyway?"

Jak knew quite well that Delacort knew the answer, but he said it anyway. "Eighty-three."

"Eighty-three." Delacort shook his head incredulously. "Eighty-three," he repeated. "You know"— and he waggled a meaty finger at Jak—"when I first started this colony . . ."

"Back in the old days," Jak said with extreme seriousness. "Back in the days before space travel, when you had to walk here from earth. Ninety million miles, in the snow. Uphill all the way."

"That's right," Delacort said gravely. "With dinosaurs nipping at our heels the entire time." He smiled briefly, and then continued. "No, seriously, Jak. When we first started things up here, there was exactly one committee. It was headed up by yours truly. And it was called the Committee to Get Things Done. And I swore that we weren't going to fall into the old trap of parceling out every damned responsibility. And you know what happened?"

"We did," said Jak.

"We did," affirmed Delacort. He waved his hands vaguely. "Well, Kolker take it. In three months I'm retiring off this rock and it's going to be all yours. Yours and your lovely bride's."

"Right. Sure you're going to retire," said Jak. "You said that last year and the year before that."

Delacort affected an air of being stricken. "What are you, disappointed that you're not rid of me?"

Jak made a dismissive gesture, and then there was a buzz at the door. "Come," Delacort called.

The doors hissed open and L'rita peeked in. She knew in what high regard Jak really held Delacort, and although Jak covered it with good-natured banter,

L'rita was too open an individual to cover her feelings in that manner. So she always acted a bit shy around Delacort.

"Is this a bad time?" she asked tentatively.

Delacort gestured for her to come in. "Not at all," he said. "I was just chatting with your victim here."

"Victim?" She blinked, not entirely getting it. L'rita was the absolute top of the heap when discussing quantum astrophysics, but subtleties such as humor and gentle sarcasm went right past her. "You mean my fiancé?"

Delacort shrugged. "Is there a difference?"

"Ignore him, honey," said Jak. He gestured for L'rita to come to him, and when she did he ran his fingers affectionately over her bald pate. He felt the slightest hint of fuzz and knew that meant she'd be shaving her head again quite soon. "What's up?"

"We just have a few last-minute things to go over for the wedding reception tonight."

"Last-minute?" said Delacort. "I'll say last-minute. If you waited any longer, you wouldn't be discussing them until after you were"—he shuddered slightly—"married. And to think that I, as head of the colony, have to perform the ceremony."

She tilted her head slightly, her pupilless black eyes studying Delacort carefully. "You react so negatively to the notion of marriage, Mr. Delacort," she said curiously. "Why?"

"An unnatural state of affairs, my dear," he boomed. "Do you know what the difference is between marriage and death?"

L'rita looked from Delacort to Jak. Not wanting to

let it dangle, Jak sighed and said, "We don't know. What's the difference, boss?"

"I don't know either," replied Delacort. "But until I've got it figured out, I'm not ready to commit myself prematurely to either one."

That was when the sirens went off.

L'rita gasped, instinctively moving closer to Jak, pressing herself against him. She looked around in confusion. "Jak?"

The air of camaraderie, of gentle banter, had evaporated in an instant. Delacort was immediately behind his computer screen once more, shouting, "Computer! Damn it, clear the screen! Give me a perimeter report!"

Jak had moved to the comm unit on the wall and was already demanding updates. At that moment the doors whooshed open without preamble, and scientists were pouring into Delacort's office like lemmings. The air was filled with the babble of voices shouting either updates of the unexpected situation or demands to know what was going on.

In the courtyard far below Delacort's office, the Klaxon continued to scream its alert, and various colonists, in assorted states of dishevelment, were staggering out into the main areas, pulling on clothes or robes to cover their nightclothes. Only crazy people like Delacort and his immediate staff were insane enough to be up and around at this hour.

Delacort was waving and shouting in irritation, "Shut up! All of you, *shut up!*" He was unable to hear the computer report, and he had to bellow, "Computer, repeat!"

"Six vessels have dropped out of warp space within the planet perimeter and are approaching the surface at accelerated speeds," said the computer voice in its deep baritone. "Preliminary sensor scans indicate their weapons are armed and ready. The general size and configurations of the vessels indicate a ninety-three percent likelihood they are the same vessels that attacked the Alpha and Beta Xaridian systems within the past four months."

"Nearest planetary defense system?" he asked.

"Bravo station."

"Direct communication link now. *Now!*" he added, as if the additional shouting would somehow speed up the computer's instantaneous communications capabilities.

A moment later a calm drawl came over the intercom. "This is Sloan at Bravo station," they heard. "You ringing me up to tell me we're having company, chief?"

Delacort drew an arm across the sweat that seemed to have materialized on his upper lip. He breathed a silent prayer of thanks to the protective spirit of Kolker. Sloan was the most experienced man they had in a planetary defense position. If they had to be under attack, they couldn't be in a better situation. "Yeah, Sloan. What've you got?"

"I'm tracking them," said Sloan. "Fast puppies . . . but nothing I can't handle. Phaser cannons are locking on. We'll have target confirmation in about four seconds."

Delacort nodded and cast a quick glance at the people crowding his office. His people. Their faces were a uniformly pasty color. He imagined that his was as well. He didn't see Jak, and he raised his voice slightly as he called out, "Jak! Get an emergency broadcast off to Starfleet! Tell them—"

"Just did it," said Jak. "Figured I should take care of it, just in—" He glanced at L'rita, whose arm was around his waist. She was trembling against him. "Just in case things get too confused later."

It was not, of course, what he was originally going to say. Delacort knew it all too well, and the unspoken completion hung there—*just in case we don't make it.*

But that wasn't going to happen.

"Talk to me, Sloan," said Delacort.

There was a long moment in which Delacort saw his life passing before him, and then Sloan's comforting voice sounded through the office. "Targets acquired," he said. "We have positive firing signatures."

Delacort's response was succinct. With what had already happened to Alpha and Beta Xaridian, no chances could be taken. No presumptions made. If the intruders even seemed to smell hostile, the only thing to do was proceed on the assumption that they *were* hostile.

He licked his lips once and said, "Blow them to hell."

"Look!"

One of the committee heads was pointing out Delacort's large bay window. Far, far to the east, they could see small balls of fire lighting up the sky. The ground phaser cannons were unleashing their armament on the incoming hostiles. Moments later the sight of the cannonfire was accompanied by the sounds, but they were coming over the comm link that the computer had established. The high-pitched

7

whine of the ground-based phaser defenses had always given Delacort a headache. Now, though, they were the sweetest sounds he'd ever heard.

And then he heard something not so sweet.

"God damn!" came Sloan's angry voice. "They're fast little buggers, I'll give 'em that! Stoner! Dini! Reacquire targets, damn it! Get them before—"

And suddenly, there at the horizon line where Bravo station was firing at the incoming vessels, a ball of fire leaped into existence and arced upward, as if trying to reach for the sky and caress it with fingers of sizzling heat. There was no sound except for a sudden burst of static that came over the comm link.

"Communications ended," the computer said with dispassionate calm.

At first there was no sound, and then Delacort managed to get out a question: "Reason for end of communication?"

"Bravo station has been destroyed."

There was barely time for the people in the office to digest that bit of information, and then they saw them—the attackers—seeming to dive straight out of the sun that was now rising. It was as if they were being spit straight out of a gateway to hell.

From toward the back, Jak spoke, in a voice that was barely above a whisper. "Del . . . what do we do?"

When Delacort replied, he felt as if it were someone else's voice. As if he were speaking from a million miles away.

"Jak—send on all frequencies, so those bastards can hear us."

"You're on, boss."

Delacort raised his voice slightly and said, "This is Administrator Delacort. Break off your attack immediately. Starfleet has been informed of your hostile activities. You do not have a chance. Reply, please."

He waited for a reply—something, anything. A boast. A threat. A demand. Something.

What he got was the screaming of air as the vessels descended. They made a low pass that shook the walls, caused the still morning air to thunder around them. The floor beneath Delacort's feet shook, and his glass and crystal pieces toppled off their mountings. The room was filled with the sound of shattering fragile things—things like sculptures, Delacort thought, and dreams.

The vessels came around, and this time, when they made their pass, they opened fire. Delacort closed his eyes, but was unable to shut his ears as the sounds of ray blasts filled the courtyard outside. From below him came the screams of his people—people whom he had been unable to protect. His office, too, was filled with screams and shouts, the thundering of feet and the stink of sweat and death. He heard buildings crack and crumble beneath the assault and went to his window, pressing himself against it as if to present the greatest possible target.

Below him the colony was in flames. He saw mothers clutching the broken bodies of their children, and then buildings collapsing forward upon them. He saw decades of his life going up in blazing ruins. Hot tears rolled down his cheeks, and when he turned he saw that his office was empty except for Jak and L'rita. Her face was buried in Jak's chest, her back shaking from racking sobs. Jak was chewing his lower lip, running his hands across her head and trying to tell her that everything, everything, was going to be all right.

Delacort stared at them.

And once again, in a voice that seemed to be coming from someone else, Delacort was speaking. "Do you, Jak, take L'rita . . . to be your lawfully wedded wife, to have and to hold till death do you part?"

They looked up at him, as if he'd lost his mind. Incredibly, he was smiling. "Well?"

"Del . . . are you—"

"I don't think we have much time," Delacort said, prodding gently.

"He does," L'rita said quickly. "And I do, too."

Jak looked down at her and a second later was kissing her hungrily, desperately, drowning in her.

"Then by the power vested in me—" said Delacort.

The window blew inward, the air frying around them. The explosion drove Delacort forward, and he wondered about the distant stinging pain in his chest. He looked down and saw the huge shard of glass projecting outward and stared at it in stupefaction before falling.

Jak took a step toward him, and then the building was hit again. This time it was no near miss. This time the ceiling exploded, and debris rained down upon him. L'rita screamed his name once and leaped into his embrace as the ceiling fell in on them completely. Then the floor under them collapsed, plunging to the ground five stories below.

For another five minutes the raiding vessels continued pounding the research colony. They made pass after pass, until they were satisfied that no life remained beneath them.

And then . . .

Then they took . . .

Nothing.

Instead the raiders circled around, their sleek triangular vessels glinting in the morning light that Delacort had so loved. They arced away toward the rising sun, leaving behind them death and destruction and no reason whatsoever for their massacre.

The emergency signal, of course, had already gone out to Starfleet. But the raiders did not particularly care about that.

They had their own concerns.

And, surrounded by death, they did part.

Chapter Two

THE COMM UNIT on Uhura's wall beeped once. She walked over to it and tapped it with the side of her hand. "Lieutenant Uhura here," she said.

"Lieutenant, a moment of your time in my quarters, to go over the final details of your mission."

"Yes, Captain," she said. "Right away."

"Take your time, Lieutenant. We don't rendezvous with the *Lexington* for another five hours."

"Yes, sir."

Walking out into the corridor, she headed for the captain's quarters, nodding or smiling to crewmen as she passed them. She had a way about her that caused people to relax almost immediately.

Abruptly she frowned as she heard something that was rather unusual in the corridors of the *Enterprise*—the sound of running feet. For a brief, giddy moment she thought that perhaps the ship was on red alert and somehow she'd simply been oblivious to the signals. But no, others passing her by heard the footsteps, too, and exchanged slightly confused glances with her.

And then, around the corner, his arms pumping furiously, sped an ensign. It was only at the last moment that he realized he was on a direct collision course with Uhura, and he pinwheeled his arms and backpedaled quickly, without allowing for his momentum. The result was that his feet shot out from under him and he hit the floor, landing bone-jarringly on his rump.

Uhura stood over him, her arms folded and her lips slightly puckered. Her instinct was to reach down and help haul him to his feet, but she intuited—correctly —that he would simply be further mortified if she aided him. He rose quickly, hurriedly brushing himself off and murmuring abject apologies.

"Are you all right?" she asked, trying to fight down her amusement.

He blinked in surprise, as if his own physical condition was of such little significance as to be completely irrelevant. "Oh. Oh, yes. Never better."

His feet were shuffling slightly, and he was clearly anxious to keep moving to wherever he was heading. But protocol required that he now stand there until the superior officer—who had acknowledged his presence—made it clear that she was done with him.

"Ensign Chekov," she said, one eyebrow slightly raised in a mannerism she'd picked up from Spock. "You're in a great hurry, Ensign. Accidents can be caused that way."

"Yes, Lieutenant," he said, bobbing his head nervously.

"Where were you off to in such a hurry?"

"The bridge, ma'am. To my post."

"Were you under the impression that you were going to miss the bridge somehow?" she asked. "That it was going to leave without you?"

"Oh, no, ma'am," he said in a very serious tone. "I did not think that at all. But I was . . . *am* . . . late reporting for duty."

"How late?"

"Forty-five seconds, ma'am," he said, and then amended, "Well . . . now a minute forty-five."

"Yes, well, you'd be even later if you broke a leg or sprained an ankle en route, Ensign," she said, fighting to keep the corners of her mouth from twitching. "Take it a bit more slowly next time."

"Yes, ma'am. I did not want the keptin to notice that—"

"The captain is in his quarters, waiting for me," said Uhura. "So he doesn't know about your . . . indiscretion."

Chekov looked at her apprehensively, and she added, "He won't hear it from me, if that's what you're thinking."

He nodded gratefully. "Thank you, ma'am."

They stared at each other for a moment, and then Uhura inclined her head slightly to indicate that Chekov should go on his way. Immediately Chekov was off, starting to dash, and then braking himself before Uhura could say anything. He walked quickly, his hands balled into fists, his feet just bordering on a run. It was clearly all he could do to contain himself.

Indeed, it was the same for Uhura, who barely was able to wait until young Chekov was gone from view before bursting into laughter.

Just as quickly as she felt cheered, she became saddened again. The casual encounter had simply underscored for her that she was about to go off and be a stranger on another ship. No matter how crowded a starship was, it could be extremely painful if it was filled with 429 strangers.

Kirk did not look up from his work when he heard the buzzer at his cabin. "Come," he said simply.

The door hissed open. He did not even have to bother to raise his gaze. There was a distinctive scent of perfume, and the slight tinkling of that particular pair of large earrings that his communications officer occasionally favored. Kirk usually had to look up to confirm the identity of a male who entered his cabin, but for females he had almost a sixth sense. "Sit down, Lieutenant," he said. "Be right with you."

Uhura, for her part, was surprised at the casual manner in which her captain was able to identify her without looking up at her.

She sat down obediently, momentarily unsure of what to do with her hands before finally resting them in her lap.

Kirk shut off the computer screen and turned to look at her. "Nervous?" he asked.

She let out a soft sigh. "A bit, Captain," she said. "Being away from home . . ."

"You don't think of Earth as home?" he asked.

She shrugged slightly. "Not for some time," she admitted. "And you, sir?"

He pursed his lips. "Not even when I was living there," he said candidly. He rose from behind his desk. "But you don't have to worry, Lieutenant. I've known Commodore Wesley for years. A good man. I might go so far as to say he's the second best starship commander in the fleet."

"Second best?" asked Uhura. "And the first . . . ?"

Kirk smiled. "What's life without mystery, Lieutenant? Take your own guess." Then the gently bantering tone evaporated, and Kirk was speaking in all seriousness. "The *Lexington* is a damned fine ship. I wouldn't be sending one of my officers there if I thought otherwise."

"With all due respect, Captain . . . you're sending me because of Starfleet orders."

Kirk shrugged slightly. "There are orders and then there are orders, Lieutenant. A captain has a certain degree of leeway when it comes to requests for personnel to be moved around. If he feels that a move is going to be contrary to the best interests of the personnel involved, he can in various official and polite ways tell Starfleet precisely what they can do with their request. With this *Lexington* business, however, I would be hard-pressed to fault either the reassignment or the reasons for requesting it."

He walked around the desk and sat on the edge of it. "Look, Lieutenant . . . nine times out of ten, your duties on *Enterprise* tap only the barest fraction of your true abilities. But these diplomatic meetings with the Rithrim that *Lexington* is involved with . . . they are really going to push you. The mixture of verbal and sign language that constitutes the Rithramen tongue is difficult for even the most ac-

17

complished diplomats to master. You, however, are one of Starfleet's premiere linguists. It's about time you had a chance to show that ability off."

"Yes, sir," she said, bobbing her head slightly. "Have we gotten any further word on what precisely it is the Rithrim want us for?"

Kirk shook his head. "No," he confessed. "Starfleet would like to build an installation for deep-space observation in Rithramen space, to replace the one that the Gorn destroyed not too long ago. Partly for observation of deep-space phenomena and partly— and no one makes any bones about this—to keep an eye on the Gorn, since the Rithrim border is so close to Gorn space. And the Rithrim, in turn, say that they're willing to talk—providing we aid them in averting some sort of danger that threatens their population. But they have yet to clarify just precisely what that danger is."

"Could that be due to the difficulty in communicating with them?" she asked.

He shrugged. "Either that or they're just being cagey. That's one of the things you're going to have to determine, Lieutenant. And since part of your pre-*Enterprise* experience involved dealing with cultures and languages similar to those employed on Rithra, Starfleet felt that you would be well suited to the job."

She didn't say anything at first, but Kirk knew something was on her mind. "Lieutenant?" he gently prodded her.

"Well, if they were so anxious to have me as part of this mission, Captain, I don't see why they didn't just assign the *Enterprise* to handle the entire thing."

"Yes, you do, Lieutenant."

She sighed. "Because Rithra is in *Lexington*'s sector, yes, sir. I know."

He looked at her, not unsympathetically. "What's really on your mind, Lieutenant?"

She looked up at him, with an air that projected strictly business. "I'm only concerned about the effect on *Enterprise* that my absence might have, Captain," she said. "Communications will be understaffed. I have good people under me, but they don't carry a great deal of experience. I wish Starfleet had given me more notice. I dislike the idea of just leaving you in the lurch, as it were."

"As it were." Kirk nodded. "Lieutenant, I think you're underestimating your own ability to train people. They'll do a fine job in your temporary absence."

"Temporary."

The way she said that word was more than enough to confirm Kirk's suspicions about the true nature of her concern. "Lieutenant," he said, assuming that slightly bigger-than-life air he put on when he was speaking in a tongue-in-cheek manner, "I get the distinct feeling that you think we're going to rent out your quarters while you're gone."

She didn't understand. "Sir?"

Kirk folded his arms across his chest. "Bob Wesley likes to refer to himself as—and I quote here—a good judge of horseflesh, unquote. Meaning that he is able to recognize some of the best and brightest officers in the fleet, and he will occasionally do what he can to wangle them onto his ship on a permanent basis. That is part of what makes the *Lexington* such an excellent vessel."

"I see."

"On the other hand," Kirk continued, "part of what makes the *Enterprise* the talk of the fleet— You do know we're the talk of the fleet, do you not, Lieutenant?"

"Oh, subspace chatter is just burning up about us, Captain," she affirmed gravely.

"Yes. And what contributes to that is the uncanny ability of the *Enterprise* captain to do the exact same thing as Commodore Wesley. Meaning, Lieutenant, that as far as I'm concerned, this is only a temporary assignment. Your place, for as long as you want it, will always be here."

She nodded gratefully. "Thank you, sir."

"We'll keep a candle burning for you in the window, Lieutenant."

"I'll be looking for it, Captain."

Upon returning to her cabin, Uhura logged on to her desktop computer and quickly scanned her personal section for messages, looking only for those she would have to answer before leaving the *Enterprise*.

To her surprise, there was a congratulatory note from Lieutenant Palmer, her number two. She sighed briefly; never a secret on this starship. Nothing else seemed urgent, and she quickly filed the messages into a buffer for retrieval after her mission.

Quickly surveying her quarters, Uhura mentally prepared her packing list, not wanting to leave anything behind. A touch of a stud on the side of her bed opened a small panel, and she deftly grabbed her Starfleet-issue carryall. Then she turned around and began opening drawers in her dresser, trying to think through the necessities for a diplomatic mission. Class-A uniform. Dress uniform. Her favorite tricorder. A handful of her music discs. Her . . . but the thought was stopped when her door beeped.

"Come," she said, thinking it was Captain Kirk with more information.

Her look of concern was quickly replaced by a smile as Lieutenant Sulu sauntered in. Making himself at home, the helmsman plopped himself on top of her neat bed next to her growing pile of belongings. He looked around the room, admiring the cultural artifacts decorating the walls and her dresser.

"Hi," he began. "I just got the word down on the rec deck and thought I'd wish you well. Word spreads pretty quickly around here, you know."

She laughed and waved an arm to move him aside. After opening the carryall, she began folding her uniforms and placing them inside it.

"Of course. Isn't that what our computer bulletin board is for? Besides, you couldn't keep a secret if your life depended on it. After all, who spilled the beans about Riley's surprise party? We all know about you, Mr. Sulu."

He smiled ruefully. "Guilty as charged. "So, what's the deal with the *Lexington?*"

"A diplomatic mission, and they need me. I'm pretty flattered. The captain told me in person instead of having Mr. Spock do it. Must be important to the Federation."

Uhura smiled as Sulu started folding her dress uniform.

"I think the captain just wanted to protect his communications officer. Commodore Wesley has two reputations: One, he's a stern commander. Two, he'll move mountains of paper through Starfleet to get a crew member he likes. That's how we nearly lost Styles and Dr. Noel, you know."

"Mere rumor," she replied, although her tone said otherwise. Walking into her other room, Uhura called out, "Would you mind grabbing my extra boots? They're under the bed."

Nodding, he placed the dress uniform gingerly inside the carryall. Sulu then reached under her bed and pulled out the extra pair of boots. Absently he began polishing them with a shirtsleeve, although they were shiny enough to begin with.

Uhura returned from the other room, her arms filled with final items for her bag. She placed those belongings in the carryall and then stared into space, quickly reviewing her mental packing list. Satisfied that all was ready, she closed the bag and placed a security code on the lock.

"When do we rendezvous?" she asked.

"Another few hours. Chekov was heading up to the bridge early to double-check the course."

"He seems like a good kid," she said, sitting beside Sulu on the bed. "Kind of nervous at times, but he certainly knows that board."

"He'll do fine. Being under the captain's scrutiny can be pretty intimidating at times."

"Then you have to loosen the boy up," she said with a smile. "After all, you'll be sitting right there with him. And just think—without me around, you can start in on him."

Sulu slowly smiled at the comment. "And just what does that mean?"

"Fencing. I'm tired of being your main sparring partner. He's younger and more impressionable than I am, so you can easily get him down to the gym. He might even think of it as an order from a senior officer."

"Thank you for your support," he said with a smile. "We'll see which one of us is more limber in our dotage. Come on, shift's going to change."

They stood together, ready to leave for the bridge. Both of them were always eager to get up there. Not only was it the hub of all activity on the ship, and a special place for both officers, but it allowed them an opportunity to be part of the decision-making process, part of the action.

For Uhura, the bridge was the beginning and end of every assignment. She was privy to Kirk's log entries and was certainly aware of who got—or didn't get—messages from loved ones. Even though there were 429 people aboard the ship, she could always sense who needed a little moral support or who should get a pat on the back.

As for Sulu, he was always the first to catch sight of the unexpected, and he could treat himself to a particularly good view of each cosmic event. He truly felt challenged guiding the massive starship through the heavens and from star to star. It was he who steered them away from trouble or toward something new and exciting.

That feeling of finding the unknown, he'd told her often enough, was what had led him to Starfleet and kept him tied to the helm after a brief stint in astrophysics. Nor would he have traded his current assignment for anything else.

Out in the corridor they walked along, nodding to the fellow crew members they knew. The place was leisurely for Sulu, steady for Uhura. He always paced himself so as not to force her to hurry.

She, in turn, always teased him about walking like an old-fashioned Earther and about needing to ease up on himself. But by now she knew it was a lost battle. Sulu was too irrepressible, too full of energy, to work at any speed slower than fast.

Still, she enjoyed being challenged by him and learning about new things. While Uhura had her music and her communications computers, he had so many other interests. There was botany for about a year and then theater, and he never stopped exercising, citing fencing as the best way to keep the reflexes sharp. The sport had its challenges, Uhura had agreed early on, though she preferred swimming for building up her muscles and endurance.

"I heard that Ensign Berganza and Lieutenant Pittarese broke up," Uhura mentioned as they stood before the turbolift doors. While it usually took less than a minute to get a lift, it always seemed to be a long wait for her.

"Too bad," Sulu noted. "I thought they were a cute couple. But you know the old saying: Never mix biophysics and astronomy." The doors swished open, revealing an empty cab.

"I never heard that before," she said as they entered the lift. She gripped the handle, turned it slightly and commanded, "Bridge."

"Of course not. You hear the best sayings down in the gym."

"Don't start with me, mister."

"Aye-aye." There was a pause; when Sulu spoke again, it was in a quieter, deeper voice. "You'll be okay out there, won't you?"

"Of course. I'm excited about the contact and about getting a juicy landing-party assignment. It doesn't sound as if there's going to be trouble."

He smiled. "Fine. Just come back. Don't let Wesley's charms lure you away."

She smiled back, appreciating his friendship. They made a good pair, but neither truly entertained romantic thoughts about the other. Sometimes a straightforward friendship was more rewarding, and Uhura cherished this one.

"I like it fine right here," she assured him. "But thanks. It's always nice to be appreciated."

"All part of the service," Sulu told her.

The doors snapped open with a soft swoosh, allowing Sulu to step out with Uhura beside him. He quickly checked the personnel, noting that it was business as usual. Spock was in the center seat, awaiting Captain Kirk's arrival; Chekov remained at navigation, hunched over his readouts; Lieutenant Leslie was over the engineering and environmental displays, and a yeoman was taking down data from the library computer.

The helmsman tapped Chekov on the shoulder as he slid himself into his seat. The ensign's head bobbed up and he smiled.

"Hello, Mr. Sulu. Ve're steady at varp two, and I've made the final course adjustments."

"Good." Sulu studied his own readouts and was satisfied that things were normal. "Another dry run to

Gamma Two after this . . . and then more mapping. Should be boring—more so without Uhura to keep things enchanting in the rec rooms."

"She does have an excellent voice," Chekov agreed. He then fell silent, worrying over his board.

"The readouts won't change anytime soon," Sulu said. "Relax a bit. We're how far from the *Lexington?*"

Chekov looked down at the astrogator. "Two hours, twenty-seven minutes."

"So they won't be in sensor range for a while. Enjoy the view." Sulu turned back to his board, checking some of his own settings.

Chekov wrung his hands to flex them and then leaned back—just a bit. Relaxing was obviously not something that came easily to him. The ensign was still very much a newcomer on board the *Enterprise,* someone who felt he had much to prove. Relaxing between ports of call was something he still had to learn, and something Sulu was determined to teach him.

The navigator looked over his shoulder and watched as Uhura settled into her seat and scanned the latest flow of information. Although messages directed just to the *Enterprise* took priority, the starship computers received and recorded hundreds of messages a day. Some were Starfleet news updates for the senior staff. Others were the steady stream of chatter coming from ships in the quadrant, personal messages for crew, and stray signals picked up by the sensor array.

Uhura's staff was quite good at sorting things out, Sulu knew, and they always kept an eye out for a juicy tidbit picked up from the strays. These were the kinds of facts that wouldn't be needed for formal reports but found their way onto the ship's bulletin boards, an area run by the rec director but aided and abetted by the communications staff.

Uhura caught him watching and smiled.

"Anything good in the ether?" Sulu asked.

"Seems quiet," she replied. "Some more border skirmishes with Klingon ships. The Vulcans have some new discovery that Mr. Spock will no doubt find 'fascinating.' And I think Angela Martine will be disappointed to learn her Meteors lost the championship magno-ball game to the Pipers."

Sulu nodded and then returned his attention to the systems checks he liked to run at the start of each shift. Finally, satisfied that his board was in order, he toggled his communicator and called down to the phaser room. Specialist Angela Martine responded cheerfully and they did a quick run-through on weapons status.

"We're showing green on the board," Martine responded at the end.

"Good." Sulu snapped off the communicator and gave some thought to Martine. She was an experienced officer who had suffered a deep blow when her fiancé, Tomlinson, died during a skirmish with the Romulans. The first contact with the Romulans in a century, Sulu mused, and Tomlinson was the only casualty. He shook his head.

Fortunately Martine had handled the situation pretty well, recovering as quickly as could be expected. She was once again one of the top weapons specialists in the fleet. But her loss had left her a little stiff in social situations.

Recently Sulu had tried to get her to loosen up with his fledgling musical theater group—but it turned out she couldn't carry a tune.

Maybe he could get her to help him with his botany garden. With Yeoman Rand no longer aboard, he needed help with the temperamental plant-form he'd named Beauregard. Yes, maybe a little relaxing botany would be good for Martine, he thought.

Unfortunately it would be a long time between thought and action.

Chapter Three

"SIR, WE ARE BEING HAILED by the *Lexington*."

Despite their talk, Uhura still sounded the slightest bit apprehensive. Kirk smiled at her as he said, "On screen, Lieutenant."

The image of the *Lexington* vanished from the viewscreen and was replaced by the visage of Commodore Wesley.

Kirk had never forgotten his first encounter with Robert Wesley—it was when Kirk was being considered for command of the *Enterprise*. Wesley had been on the review board and had been the most vocal in stating that James T. Kirk was too young to receive such an important assignment. "Despite all the education that Starfleet Academy can provide," Wesley had stated, "the greatest single teacher that our officers can learn from is experience. And in that respect James Tiberius Kirk is sorely deficient."

But Wesley had been outvoted—he had, in fact, been the lone holdout—as the rest of Wesley's associates had been mightily impressed by all that Kirk had accomplished in his relatively short time as a Starfleet officer. His performance at the Academy had been faultless; the recommendations from such luminaries as Matt Decker, who had had dealings with Kirk since the would-be captain's days as an Academy plebe, and Kirk's subsequent commanding officers; the knack for original thinking that such already legendary maneuvers as Kirk's performance on the Kobayashi Maru test had already proven—all had been factored into the decision to give Kirk the *Enterprise* command.

And it was Wesley who had delivered the news to him. Hell, the commodore had insisted on it. For Wesley, who had fought the assignment, wanted to make it clear to the novice captain that—now that the decision had been made—Wesley had every intention of honoring and supporting it, and dealing with Kirk just as he did with any other starship captain.

"We are a fraternity, Kirk," he had said. "A brotherhood. Brothers can disagree with each other, but the bottom line is that we have to support each other. We have to trust each other. Because trust is something that Starfleet runs on, and if we don't have that, then pretty damned soon we don't have a fleet. Follow?"

Kirk had nodded and shaken Wesley's hand and found that the towering commodore's firm opinions were backed up by an even firmer handshake. So firm, in fact, that Kirk fancied he could feel the bones cracking in his fingers.

That had been only a few years ago, and yet when

Wesley nodded at him on the viewscreen, it seemed an eternity ago. "Captain Kirk," said Wesley.

"Commodore," replied Kirk with a brief inclination of his head.

"Is Lieutenant Uhura prepared to come aboard the best starship in the fleet?" Wesley asked.

"No, Commodore," replied Kirk evenly. "She's prepared to leave it."

A grin split Wesley's face. "Touché, Captain."

"The commodore's reputation precedes him," Kirk said, interlacing his fingers. "Actually, Bob, I'm a-mazed you're out this far. Usually you can be found hanging around the exit door of the Academy saying, 'I'll take that one, that one, and that one.'"

"Now, now, Jim," Wesley replied, waggling a scolding finger. "A few good people still slipped through my net. I've heard good things about Riley."

"One of my more colorful junior officers," Kirk deadpanned. Although Kirk had been generous enough to keep the details of his various officers' behavior during the recent Psi 2000 incident out of the official log, he still couldn't think of Riley without remembering endless choruses of "I'll Take You Home Again, Kathleen," piped over the ship's intercom. It wouldn't have been so bad if Riley had sung on key.

Wesley was ticking off names on his fingers. "And Kyle is a top transporter man. And M'Benga . . . well, from what I understand, they refer to him as the new McCoy."

"I'm sure that will come as news to the real McCoy," said Kirk, turning an amused glance at

Spock. The Vulcan, unsurprisingly, made no comment.

Wesley seemed to squint slightly. "Who's that stalwart-looking fellow over there?"

He was indicating the *Enterprise* bridge tactical station. A square-jawed man with dark gray hair looked up in surprise, then glanced at Kirk.

"That's Security Chief Giotto," said Kirk.

"I like the cut of his jib," Wesley told him. "Put him on the list, too."

"Bob, are you giving me your Christmas wish list here?"

"Just admiring your people, Captain."

"Admire them from afar, if you don't mind, Commodore."

The tongue-in-cheek banter was abruptly interrupted when Uhura suddenly turned to Kirk. "Captain," she said. "Receiving a communication from Starfleet. We—" She interrupted herself and said, "You are to report to the Xaridian systems. Details to follow."

"Xaridian," Wesley said, all hints of joking immediately dropped. "It's where they're having that problem with raiders, isn't it?"

"That's my understanding," Kirk affirmed.

"Be damned careful, Jim," said Wesley. "From what I hear, those raiders are pretty nasty customers." He paused a moment, seeming to consider possibilities. "We're going to be practically breathing on the Gorn's scales once we get to Rithra. If there's going to be a nasty reception, we should know about it. What are the odds that these Xaridian raiders are with the Gorn?"

Kirk swiveled in his chair to face Spock. The Vulcan science officer needed no further prodding. "Ever since the difficulties began, we have been studying the methods of the raiders' attacks. They do not fit the profiles of the Gorn . . . or, for that matter, those of the Klingons or Romulans. It would appear that they are not individuals with whom we've had much contact."

"And from that we can surmise . . . ?" asked Kirk.

Spock cocked his head slightly. "Not a great deal at this time."

"Once you have the full particulars from Starfleet, please send us the information on a coded frequency," said Wesley. "I'd like to be kept apprised of the situation."

"What are you thinking, Bob?" Kirk asked slowly. "That somehow the Rithra business is connected with the raiders?"

"I don't know," Wesley admitted. "There's no rational reason to assume that."

"None whatsoever. The two systems are nowhere near each other. And the Rithrim haven't reported any raids."

"Nonetheless," said Wesley, allowing some of his frustration to show through, "the Rithrim have been so damned vague about everything, their request could be about almost anything."

"In that event, you be certain to keep *us* apprised," Kirk said. "And I'm sure I can trust you to do so, Commodore. After all, you'll have the best communications officer in the fleet on your ship."

"Ah, yes. Lieutenant Uhura." Wesley inclined his

head slightly in her direction. "It will be a pleasure to have you working with us."

"The pleasure is mine, Commodore," she said, rising from her station.

"Uhura . . . you'd better be on your way," said Kirk, hoping he didn't sound peremptory. They were wasting too much time on social niceties.

"Just a few last-minute things, Captain," Uhura said.

"Anything Lieutenant Palmer can't handle?"

Uhura looked at the blond woman who had already arrived on the bridge. She had been on alert to report there as soon as the *Lexington* came within range. Palmer raised her eyebrows, as if curious whether there was something Uhura thought she could not deal with.

"No, sir," said Uhura.

"All right, then," said Kirk. "Good luck, Lieutenant. We'll be seeing you back here soon."

"Aye, sir."

Kirk turned back to Wesley as Uhura exited into the turbolift. "The lieutenant is on her way, Bob. She should be aboard within three minutes."

"Good. We both have other business to attend to."

"Commodore—"

"Yes, Captain?"

Kirk regarded Wesley with a tolerant look. "None of the formidable Commodore Wesley charm. You can be a very pleasant taskmaster."

"I'll take that as a compliment," said Wesley.

"Whatever you wish," Kirk said agreeably. "But I'd like Lieutenant Uhura back, if you don't mind."

"Well"—and Wesley smiled broadly—"that will be up to the lieutenant, now, won't it? *Lexington* out."

Wesley's image vanished as the *Lexington* reappeared. The ship waited only long enough to confirm the beaming over of Uhura before pivoting and shooting into warp space. Kirk watched them go as Sulu turned in his chair.

"Captain," he said, his curiosity piqued, "do you think there's a chance that Lieutenant Uhura will choose to remain on *Lexington?*"

Kirk stared at Sulu for a moment and then made a sweeping gesture that encompassed the entirety of the bridge.

"And give up all this?" he asked incredulously.

Uhura and Commodore Wesley materialized side by side on the *Lexington*'s main transporter platform. She was holding her duffel bag in one hand, despite the commodore's gallant offer to carry it for her.

She looked around—at the room itself and at the woman behind the transporter console. There was something disconcerting about seeing someone other than Kyle or Scotty there, but she took it in stride.

You're not on the *Enterprise* now, she reminded herself. And you're not reporting to Captain Kirk. There are bound to be a few differences.

Just as she and Wesley stepped down from the platform, the doors whispered open and a couple of blue-shirted officers came through them. One was muscular and athletic-looking, with dark hair and a reddish-brown beard. The other was tall and bony, with pale skin and hair the color of straw.

"Ah," said Wesley dryly. "Better late than never."

The bearded man regarded him. "Sorry, sir. A last-minute course correction. Seems there's a series of comets in Beta Ganymede." Turning to Uhura, he grinned through his beard and held out his hand. "Good to have you aboard, Lieutenant. The name's Samuels—Wynn Samuels."

"Mr. Samuels is my first officer," Wesley noted. "And a damned good one at that." He indicated the tall man. "I'd also like you to meet Peder Coss, my ship's surgeon."

Coss trained his piercing blue eyes on the newcomer. "Welcome to the *Lexington*," he said, his voice deep and a little harsh-sounding, though his smile seemed warm enough.

"Thank you," Uhura told him, returning the smile. "I look forward to working with both of you gentlemen."

"Good," said Wesley. "Now that that's settled, I'm sure Lieutenant Uhura would like to unpack. Mr. Samuels, I'd appreciate it if you'd see the lieutenant to her quarters. The doctor and I have some business to conduct in sickbay."

The first officer's brows came together in what seemed like genuine concern. "Business, sir? Anything I should be aware of?"

Wesley sighed. "A physical," he replied, so softly Uhura could barely hear him.

Samuels's eyes crinkled ever so slightly at the corners. "I'm sorry, Commodore, I didn't quite catch that. Did you say a physical?"

Wesley frowned. "You know I did, Mr. Samuels.

And I don't appreciate the sarcasm." But his voice told Uhura he didn't mind it a whole lot, either.

Coss placed a hand on the commodore's shoulder. "Tell me," he asked Uhura. "Have you ever seen a commanding officer who so absolutely refuses to look after his health?"

Uhura suppressed a grin for Wesley's sake. "As a matter of fact, Doctor, it's not an entirely foreign concept to me."

The commodore turned to Coss. "You see?" he remarked. "Kirk's probably even harder to corral than I am."

The communications officer nodded. "I wouldn't be surprised, sir."

Wesley regarded her warmly. "You know," he said, "you haven't been here two minutes, Lieutenant, and you've already helped me more than you know. This could be the beginning of a beautiful working relationship."

Uhura inclined her head slightly. "Glad to be of service, sir."

The commodore grunted appreciatively and followed the doctor out of the transporter room. Uhura turned to Samuels; he returned the scrutiny with a sunny cheerfulness to which she couldn't help but respond.

"I hope we haven't offended your sense of decorum," said the first officer. "We just like to have a little fun around here. It makes the time go faster."

Uhura shook her head. "You haven't offended me at all," she assured him. "In fact, it makes me feel right at home. Speaking of which . . ."

"I hear you," he said. "Follow me."

And without any further ado, he led the way to her quarters.

In the conference room, Sulu dropped down into the seat next to McCoy and was unable to avert his glance as he saw McCoy studying records off a medical tricorder. The name on the file surprised him.

"Chekov?" he asked. "Does Mr. Chekov have a medical problem, Doctor?"

McCoy glanced at Sulu, clearly hesitating a moment as to whether he should reprimand the helmsman for prying, however unintentionally, into the private circumstances of others. But then he considered how closely Sulu was working with the young navigator—the helmsman and the navigator had to work as much in harmony as did a doctor and a nurse during surgery. If anyone had a vested interest in the Russian, it was Sulu. Mentally and physically, McCoy shrugged.

"Nothing major," he said. "Just his routine preliminary physical. If anything, he's unduly nervous."

"Nervous?" Sulu frowned. "About something one of us said or did?"

Of course, McCoy realized what Sulu was really saying: "Was it something *I* did?" The ship's surgeon shook his head. "Not necessarily. Chekov is just driven to succeed. He wants to impress everyone immediately, and he keeps trying to come up with ways to do it. But he's not sure precisely how to go about it, and gets that much jumpier because he doesn't have any guaranteed methods."

Coming in on the tail end of the conversation were

Scotty and Security Chief Giotto. Scotty glanced from McCoy to Sulu. "Who's jumpy? Who're we talking about?"

"We are not talking about anyone," McCoy said stiffly.

"Ensign Chekov," Sulu told them.

McCoy rolled his eyes. "Why don't we just broadcast it all over the damned ship?"

"Are ye sure that would be wise, Doctor?" Scotty deadpanned. "Ye think it's everybody's business?"

"No, I don't think it's everybody's business!" McCoy said in exasperation. "I don't think it's *anybody's* business!"

"Well, Doctor, ye were the one suggesting we broadcast it."

"I wasn't suggesting that!"

"I beg your pardon, Doctor," said Giotto, "but I heard you. We all did."

Heads all around the table nodded in agreement as McCoy's head sagged into his hands. At that moment Kirk and Spock entered.

Kirk looked at the bobbing heads around the table. "It's nice to see you all in agreement on something. Anyone care to tell me what that might be?"

Sulu spoke up helpfully. "That Dr. McCoy shouldn't broadcast to the ship that Ensign Chekov is jumpy."

For a fleeting moment McCoy looked as if he wanted to slug him.

Kirk looked at McCoy, appalled. "Were you going to do that, Bones?"

"No!"

"Aye, we talked him out of it," Scotty said proudly.

"What does Chekov have to be jumpy about?" Kirk asked.

McCoy huffed, "Maybe he's worried he'll become an officer and lose his mind, like most of the men at this table."

Spock appeared to consider this. "If Ensign Chekov is worried about his psychological stability, he should seek out the chief medical officer for assistance. Then again . . . perhaps he is worried, Doctor, that you might broadcast his concerns throughout the ship."

"That would make *me* jumpy," Giotto affirmed.

"I'm going to kill somebody," McCoy said.

"Precisely the kind of declaration any crew member wishes to hear from a ship's chief medical officer," Spock observed.

McCoy shot him a lethal stare.

"Gentlemen," said Kirk, "before we further examine the undoubtedly vital question of Mr. Chekov's jumpiness, I think we'd best address the reason for this conference: the attacks on the Xaridian system. Mr. Spock?"

Spock immediately brought up on the computer screen the Starfleet dossier on the attacks. Not that he truly needed it; he had already committed the information to his formidable memory. But the Vulcan was efficient enough to want to have all the information handy in the unlikely event of his memory becoming faulty.

"The attack on the Gamma Xaridian colony was the most recent of three attacks on the Xaridian systems," Spock said. "The first was on Alpha Xaridian Two several weeks ago, and Beta Xaridian Six was next, barely a week later."

"Alpha, Beta, Gamma," said McCoy. "Am I the only one here noticing a pattern?"

"I think it is somewhat self-evident, Doctor," Spock said dryly. "All of the inhabited planets in the Xaridian systems are colony worlds. The attacks in the Alpha and Beta systems left a handful of survivors. The attack on Gamma Xaridian Three did not; the patrol ship *Viking* has already inspected that site, and the crew found no survivors."

"The bastards are getting more efficient," said Giotto.

"Crudely put, Mr. Giotto," said Spock, "but accurate. Local authorities and small ships such as the *Viking* are insufficient for the job at hand."

"Which is where we come in," said Kirk. "Descriptions of the raiders, Mr. Spock?"

"Reports vary. Some survivors sighted four ships; others saw seven," said Spock. "These ships were extremely maneuverable, extremely deadly; they appeared to fire with impunity on their targets, and none of the raiders has ever been captured or, to the best of our knowledge, so much as inconvenienced by conventional ground defenses. The scant details in the single broadcast from Gamma Xaridian were consistent with other reports."

"Can we take them?" asked Kirk.

Scotty snorted in disbelief that the subject would even be broached. "They're cowards," he said disdainfully. "Hit-and-run techniques and guerrilla tactics. They won't last five minutes against a real opponent like the *Enterprise.*"

"A foe with ships described as maneuverable and deadly, Mr. Scott, is not one whom I would hold in such open contempt," Spock said. "These raiders can dodge phaser fire and photon torpedoes, and they can batter our shields. Ultimately the *Enterprise* could be as vulnerable as any of the colonies."

Scotty said nothing, but his expression clearly showed that he disagreed with Spock's assessment of the situation.

"Contact *Viking*," Kirk said. "Make certain that they relay their findings to us. Mr. Sulu, which colony will we encounter first, given our present heading?"

"Alpha Xaridian Two, sir. The colony that was attacked first."

"Very well. Go to warp five, and inform the colonists that we'll be arriving in . . . ?"

Sulu didn't even pause. "Eleven hours."

Kirk nodded. Sulu's ability to predict ETA at any given point, at any given speed, was nothing short of amazing. "Eleven hours. Mr. Spock, I want a list of colonies that have yet to be visited by these raiders. Determine, if possible, which of them faces the greatest likelihood of being the next target.

"Mr. Scott, check the sensor arrays and tricorders. Expand the normal search radius to include some of the unusual ranges in electromagnetic and subspace spectra. If there's any unusual signature to these ships, I want to know about it.

"Mr. Sulu, we're not on yellow alert, but if the raiders show up while we're around, I want this ship to switch to a defensive posture in no time at all."

Kirk quickly scanned the room. "Do we all understand our assignments, gentlemen?"

There were nods around the table. And then Kirk

fixed McCoy with a stare. There was just the barest hint of amusement in his eyes as he added, "And, Bones . . . try not to broadcast any of this, okay?"

McCoy turned and looked at Sulu, who had started the whole thing. "I am never going to discuss a medical situation with you again—and that includes your own." He stood up and added, "And you can broadcast that!"

As Uhura entered the cabin assigned to her, she did a double take. Looking around, she saw a space much larger than she'd expected, furnished with altogether too much furniture.

These were VIP quarters, not crew accommodations. Obviously somebody had goofed. And she hadn't picked it up when she'd gotten her room assignment because the residential corridors of every starship were set up a little differently.

With a sigh, Uhura dropped her duffel on the floor and crossed to the intercom grid on the bulkhead. After tapping the appropriate stud, she called up to the first officer's station on the bridge.

"Samuels," came the response.

"Mr. Samuels, this is Lieutenant Uhura. I think there's been a mistake. I've been assigned a guest suite."

There was a brief pause as the first officer traced the source of her communication, brought up the cabin assignment listing on his monitor, and compared the two.

"No," he said finally. "No mistake. In fact, the commodore assigned you those quarters *personally*."

Uhura shook her head. "I don't get it."

Samuels grunted. "It's his way of trying to make you feel comfortable, Uhura. At home, you might say."

"Ah," she said. *"Now* I get it. Thanks, Samuels."

"Don't mention it," he told her, and ended the communication.

Uhura couldn't help but smile a little. Wesley had promised Captain Kirk he wouldn't try to steal her away—but it seemed the commodore's definition of "stealing" left room for a wide range of interpretations.

Not that she had any objection to being romanced this way. What woman would? But no amount of flattery would induce her to leave the *Enterprise,* and that was that.

She picked up her duffel and brought it back to the sleeping area in the rear of the cabin. Then, after swinging it up onto a synthetic wood cabinet, she began to unpack. Uhura had filled two of the three drawers before she realized the wood wasn't synthetic at all.

It was *real.* Delighted, she ran her fingers over its grained surface. It was unexpectedly sensual.

Maybe there *were* some advantages to serving under a commodore.

Abruptly she heard a soft, almost musical beeping. Even the door alarm sounded better in here, she noted. Emerging from behind the mesh barrier that defined her sleeping area, she said: "Come on in."

The door slid aside, revealing a tall, slender man with skin the same color as hers. His eyes were hard and black, like pieces of obsidian, and his prominent cheekbones gave his face a certain . . . what? Nobility? Or hauteur?

Inclining his head slightly, he introduced himself. "Jerome Baila. I'm the communications officer."

Uhura had heard more enthusiasm from Mr. Spock. She inclined her head in turn. "Uhura. I'm with the *Enterprise*."

He nodded. "Yes. I know." And then: "Uhura means 'freedom,' doesn't it?"

"Why, yes. How did you—" She came up with the answer to her own question. "You're Bantu."

Baila shrugged. "More or less."

Uhura started to inquire further—and then stopped herself. The man's response hadn't exactly invited further conversation on that point.

Baila took in the accommodations. "Not half bad," he judged. "Looks like Wesley's rolling out the red carpet for you."

Suddenly she realized how all this might look to him. Uhura felt the blood rush to her face.

"Lieutenant," she said, "I wasn't brought here to replace you, if that's what you're thinking. This is just an ad hoc assignment. When it's over, I'm history— believe me."

Baila smiled humorlessly. "Really," he responded. "Really."

"That may be your take on it—but I don't think it's Commodore Wesley's." A beat. "You see, the commodore and I haven't seen eye to eye lately. I wouldn't put it past him to do a little recruiting."

There was an undercurrent of resentment—of

bitterness—in Baila's voice. And though she didn't know him well enough to be sure, Uhura had a feeling it went beyond his apparent feud with Wesley.

"Well," she said, "I can't speak for the commodore, but as far as I'm concerned, I've already got a job—on the *Enterprise*."

That seemed to take some of the edge off Baila's hostility. He nodded. "Fine. In any case, we should talk about the Rithrim." Looking past her to her sleeping area and her half-full duffel, he frowned. "That is, when you're ready."

"I'm ready now," she assured him. "Though I'd prefer to have this discussion in"—she searched for the right words, found them—"less *controversial* surroundings. All right with you?"

He shrugged. "Whatever you say . . . Lieutenant."

Chekov was thankful that the captain had given the bridge crew a fifteen-minute break so that they could eat something in the mess hall before resuming their duties. After all, if things got tense, no one was going to eat anything for a while, and without food some people might be distracted.

Wiping sandwich crumbs from his hands, Chekov sat back in his chair and surveyed the room. Everyone seemed to be speculating about the current mission. He certainly had his ideas, but he didn't feel comfortable offering them to crew members he barely knew.

Uhura had assured him more than once that he'd meet everyone before long. That gave him cold comfort now, since he didn't see anyone he really knew in the room. Well, he corrected himself, he did know Sulu and Lieutenant Palmer, the relief communications officer. But he'd just finished a stint on the bridge with them and didn't want them to think he was a leech.

He watched as Sulu silently caught the eye of Lieutenant Peterson, a new officer assigned to the shuttle deck. The auburn-haired woman smiled back and gave him a small wave. It occurred to Chekov that Sulu had met Lieutenant Peterson only once or twice before, but here he was having a grand old time flirting while a dangerous mission was shaping up.

Such self-confidence, he thought; it was something he lacked. He became aware of the tension that pervaded his body and willed himself to relax. If he tensed up during a stupid meal, what could he expect during a red alert? Muscle cramps? Apoplexy?

After finishing his drink, Chekov disposed of his dishes and walked out of the mess room as casually as he could. He proceeded slowly toward the turbolift; a moment later he found him being whisked up to the bridge.

Once there, however, he started. Somehow, Sulu had managed to beat him back to their post.

"Welcome back, Pavel," Sulu said brightly.

"Thanks," Chekov acknowledged, with no little surprise in his voice. He restrained himself from asking how the helmsman had managed that trick.

Seating himself at the navigation console, he quickly called for a standard systems diagnostic. The green telltale flashed within seconds and he nodded slightly, pleased that nothing was wrong.

Next to Chekov, Sulu worked hard on his own system checks. Neither had spoken a word since returning to work. Not unusual, as the crew prepared for potential problems. Chekov found himself running his diagnostics repeatedly, keeping his head bowed.

"Something wrong, Chekov?" Sulu asked.

The Russian shook his head. "I just vant to make sure. After all, ve have no idea vhat ve're going to find."

"Probably nothing, at this point. If your board meets with your satisfaction, then let it be."

"Are you sure there's nothing out there now?" Chekov took his hands off the controls, but his eyes kept scanning the displays.

"You can see for yourself that long-range sensors show nothing unusual." There was a pause. Then, quietly, Sulu asked, "Are you worried about something?"

"Not vorried, exactly. It's just that ve might find the raiders who destroyed the colonies, and ve know nothing about them. Just how powerful are they? Vhat are they after? Can ve stop them?"

"Good questions, Ensign." Chekov spun in his chair and saw Captain Kirk standing in front of the turbolift surveying the crew.

Satisfied with what he saw, Kirk moved down to his chair. "In fact, Mr. Chekov, they're *very* good questions." He turned to Spock. "Status?"

"Sensors show no signs of disturbance," the Vulcan replied. He moved from his station to the captain's chair just as a yeoman brought Kirk the fuel-consumption report.

Kirk looked at the data padd, signed it, and returned it to the young yeoman. Turning to Spock, he sighed. "Why do I always get the fuel-consumption report *before* we go into action? If there was a problem, Scotty would be crying about his 'bairns' by now."

"Given the nature of the matter and antimatter supplies and the dilithium crystals, it would be logical to review our fuel status prior to entering into anything beyond the normal."

Kirk looked at Spock and realized rhetorical questions still went over the Vulcan's head. Figuratively biting his tongue, he just nodded and looked at the viewscreen. The stars streaked by in warp space, and there was a peaceful look to them. Once more into the unknown, he mused, and decided it was time to prepare not only himself but the bridge crew as well.

Looking at the personnel, Kirk realized that he had been in few tense situations with Chekov, who seemed so young, or with Lieutenant Palmer, despite her being ranked number two at communications.

And Chekov was right. There were a lot of unanswered questions—too many for the captain's liking.

"Let's review what we know about these raiders we're after," he said in a louder than usual voice. This made the crew pause at their stations, giving Kirk their immediate attention.

"We know that the attacks appear to be random," Spock replied. "Also, we know that the raiders will not hesitate to take lives."

The captain nodded. "Fortunately our shields are a lot stronger than the colonies'."

Sulu spoke up. "Sir, is it possible that the raiders—whoever they are—have a justifiable reason for their actions?

Kirk shrugged. "It's always possible, Lieutenant. And of course we'll hear them out. But we will *not* let them endanger any more lives." He looked around the bridge, but no one seemed to have anything else to contribute.

Finally his gaze settled on Chekov. "Ensign, *your* opinion of the situation."

The young Russian turned in his seat. He seemed pale as he replied. "With all due respect, sir, I don't think we can accomplish anything by speculating. We von't really learn anything until we find the ships."

Kirk didn't comment on the ensign's reply. He merely turned to the communications station—and was mildly surprised to see Palmer there instead of Uhura.

Damn. Not having Uhura was going to take some getting used to.

"Lieutenant Palmer," he said, "did the colonies attempt to communicate with the raiders?"

Palmer quickly lowered her earpiece and looked at the captain with bright eyes. "All reports from the colonies show their universal translators were operational. Apparently the attackers weren't much for conversation."

Chapter Four

KIRK, SPOCK, CHEKOV, AND MCCOY beamed down into the middle of the ruined colony and, apparently, the middle of a loud argument.

The second thing that Kirk noticed was the smell of something burning. He turned in a slow circle, surveying the site of Alpha Xaridian II.

At present there was nothing burning at all. But there hung in the air a sort of omnipresent blackness, a charnel stench that had not yet dissipated. It took Kirk a few moments to realize that the smell resulted partly from the fact that the raiders had managed to hit power plants, and the resultant conflagration had left the air so severely fouled that the odor remained even after the fires had been extinguished. That stench had blended with the gag-inducing smell of burned human flesh.

He looked at McCoy. The doctor had been present at any number of scenes of devastation, and he had naturally managed, like any accomplished physician, to assume an air of detachment. But McCoy was such a lover of humanity and of life that Kirk could see that such a mind-set continued to be a struggle for him.

Spock, naturally, was impassive. Kirk noticed that Chekov appeared to be the most shaken of all. That was to be expected. He made no comment on it, but instead said simply, "Mr. Chekov . . . you're with Mr. Spock. Check the ruins out for what you can find."

Spock nodded. He flipped open his tricorder and, without a word, headed toward a section of ruins to begin his inspection. Chekov joined him and then, following Spock's order, moved toward a separate section of the rubble to begin his investigation.

There was no shortage of ruins to choose from. There was, in fact, almost nothing but ruins. All over were charred and shattered buildings, smashed vehicles. Over to Kirk's right, a sign had come through unscathed that read: Botanical Gardens. Affixed to the sign was a small hand-made award cut out of blue paper. On it someone had written "1st Prize" in a childish scrawl. Kirk wondered about the story behind that award and about the quality of the gardens that had inspired some child to carefully craft the citation. Of the gardens, nothing remained except a few stumps of trees that might have stretched hundreds of feet in the air. There was charred wood and scorched ground everywhere he looked. Off to one side were the remains of a bush, which appeared to be all that was left of a very complex topiary. What its full shape had been in its prime, Kirk hadn't a clue.

Some of the buildings had been cleared away, and the skeletons of replacements were being erected. But the work was far from finished.

The loud argument going on nearby, Kirk realized, was part of some sort of town meeting. The captain looked at McCoy and inclined his head slightly in that direction. McCoy hesitated. "Didn't they know we were coming down?" he asked. The *Enterprise* doctor had grown accustomed to getting some sort of reception upon arriving planetside. Being totally ignored in favor of a loud and boisterous argument was a new experience for him.

"We told them," Kirk confirmed. "Their administrator—a fellow named Jeff Gelb—said, in essence, 'Come down if you want to. We're busy. Don't expect us to make time for you.'"

"Looks like he meant it."

They made their way toward the edge of the gathering, which numbered about twenty. Everyone was shouting at the same time. One man was calling for silence and not getting it. Kirk noted that he was lean and haunted-looking, with a scraggly brown beard.

Kirk and McCoy exchanged glances. Then Kirk filled his lungs with air and, utilizing all his inherent powers of command, bellowed, *"Quiet!"*

Whether it was the abrupt introduction of a new voice or the authority that Kirk projected or the fact that he was simply louder than everyone else . . . it worked. The bickering ceased immediately, to be replaced by a very soft and confused buzz as the colonists sought and found the source of the order.

The bearded man looked at Kirk with a degree of grudging gratitude. "Captain Kirk?"

"Mr. Gelb?" Kirk replied.

Gelb nodded briskly.

"This is our ship's doctor, Leonard McCoy. First things first—do you require medical assistance?"

"We require Starfleet to do something other than just come in after we've had the crap kicked out of us!" shouted someone in the crowd.

Kirk didn't even look in the direction of the protester. He knew it was important, in a situation like this, to deal only with the acknowledged head of the group. Otherwise the entire scene could quickly deteriorate into chaos. "Mr. Gelb," he said again, very slowly, "do you require medical assistance?"

"No, Captain," said Gelb. He had stepped up onto a pile of rubble, and now he took a step down. "We've treated those who could be treated and buried the rest. And although I would not have expressed it so rudely" —he stressed the last word and paused a moment before continuing—"we are truly in need of Starfleet's help."

"We need to get off this planet and out of this system is what we need!" someone shouted.

"This is our home!" came a reply. "Are we going to be chased out of our home by terrorists?"

"This isn't home! It's a burned-out shell!"

"We can reclaim it!"

"We should move someplace safer!"

"There is no safe place."

The last statement came not from any of the colonists but from Kirk. "Nowhere is safe," he said again, more quietly but with no less conviction.

One of the colonists—a short, belligerent-looking

man—stepped forward. "Starfleet is supposed to make it safe!" he said.

"Starfleet makes it safer," said Kirk. "But to live is to face hazards every day. If you want utter safety, climb into a sensory deprivation capsule and live your life cut off from humanity—and even then, a building could fall on you or a groundquake could open up under you and swallow you. Or an undetected blood clot could cause you to drop dead on the spot, with no warning, at any time. The only safety in life is death."

The colonists looked at one another, puzzled. Gelb cleared his throat. "Captain . . . is that somehow intended to make us feel better?"

"It's intended to let you know that colonists are the hardiest, most defiant breed there is," said Kirk. "The type who not only aren't afraid of life but are willing to challenge it directly and meet whatever challenges it might throw at them."

There was silence for a moment, and then the short man gestured toward the ruined colony and said, "This isn't difficulties. This is cold-blooded murder. They came flying in here and slaughtered us. Women, children—all died screaming. The work of years— destroyed in seconds. And I want to know what in bloody hell *you* are going to *do* about it."

Kirk looked at the faces surrounding him, full of anguish, full of fear, wanting to believe that something would happen for them, but afraid of what further might happen to them. They had fearlessly taken on the challenges that a strange planet could throw at them, but this . . . this devastation, this wanton and murderous violence . . .

Kirk's jaw twitched and his eyes narrowed. When he met the gaze of the colonists again, there was an angry fire in his eyes.

"We're going to nail those bastards to the wall," he said.

McCoy blinked in surprise, but said nothing.

"We're counting on you, Captain," Gelb said after a long moment of silence.

Kirk nodded once and then turned and walked off toward Spock. McCoy followed close on his heels and said in a low voice as Kirk took quick strides, "That's a tall order, Jim. We can't be everywhere. If the raiders show up here while we're elsewhere, the colonists will—"

"Die cursing my name," Kirk said. He looked once again at McCoy. "We're going to get them, Bones. This . . . brutality is not going to happen in my sector. I will not permit it. I will not."

McCoy said nothing. Somehow he felt that that was the only thing he could say.

Spock was crouched over one severely carbon-scored area, studying his tricorder readings and making adjustments. Kirk came up behind him and said tersely, "Report, Mr. Spock."

If Spock noticed the edge in his captain's voice, he gave no indication of it. "Curious, Captain. Preliminary tricorder readings indicate atypical residual radiation." He rose, straightening his shirt slightly. "It would seem to indicate a weapons technology unfamiliar to our science."

"How will it do against our shields?"

"I am unable to determine that at this time. Are you anticipating battle, Captain?"

56

Kirk looked at Spock coldly.

"I'm counting on it," he said.

Stalking through one of the colony's burned-out buildings, Chekov scanned the place with his tricorder. The air was thick with smoke and dust, and a number of small fires added to the black haze that hid the sky. As he approached a cabinet, his tricorder showed him something unusual and he stopped suddenly. Crouching, he reached for the cabinet door, grabbed the handle, and swung it open.

Despite the tricorder reading that had tipped him off, he was shocked to find a boy inside—a boy who had sought refuge in the cabinet. The grimace on his face told Chekov that the youth had been asphyxiated.

Chekov took a ragged breath and lifted the body out of its hiding place. After gently stretching it out on the floor, he turned away and bit back the tears.

Damn. So much destruction, so much waste. Images of what they'd found at the other colonies flooded his mind unbidden. He shook his head.

None of his training missions had prepared him for anything like this. In fact, the only scenes of devastation he had seen were in historical briefings on the old Federation-Romulan wars or the classic Russian Revolution of 1917. It had just never occurred to him that this would be a part of his Starfleet experience.

He wanted to travel among the stars, sure enough— but there was definitely a downside to exploration, and this was it. Stepping cautiously around the rubble, he couldn't help but glance back at the boy.

People weren't supposed to be blasted by beings from space—that was the stuff of old Earth stories.

Who would want to make that gruesome fiction a reality? Part of him wanted to grasp a phaser, just to feel secure that this kind of attack would not happen to him.

Instead, Chekov raised his tricorder, forcing himself to recalibrate its sensor pickup to find more examples of the radiation Spock had detected earlier. The best samples were to be gathered and beamed up to the *Enterprise* for forensic inspection. His fingers, slick with sweat, slipped twice before he finally got the adjustments right.

Bending low, Chekov waved the tricorder in front of a burned-out gray street lamp. The reading was too low to be useful. This is good, he thought. This is making me concentrate. Chekov liked puzzles, and this kind of work was good for him; it kept him interested in minutiae and how everything formed a larger picture.

He walked several meters away and then bent again, this time aiming the tricorder at a small storage building. The radiation and spectrographic readings were within the range specified by Spock. The source of the radiation was a small portable computer that had apparently been near a direct hit. Perhaps the memory was still intact, Chekov mused.

The ensign knelt to study the device more closely and gave some thought to the kind of beings who would slaughter an entire population so far inside Federation boundaries. Surely they must have realized this would bring about some sort of Starfleet action. What could the stakes be? So far no one, not even Captain Kirk, had a theory.

Unfortunately the computer's memory had been

wiped clean. Chekov rose and started back toward the beaming site.

As he walked among the blackened shells of buildings, his mind turned back a few months to his graduation from Starfleet Academy. With his high grades in just about everything, it had been a certainty he'd find a berth aboard a starship, but he had not known which one.

He would have settled for any one of the twelve Constitution-class vessels currently commissioned, although his preference was definitely the *Enterprise*. It had a unique legacy, stretching back through the heroic captaincy of Christopher Pike to the command of the legendary Captain Robert April.

Even more impressive, however—at least to Chekov—was the ship's current captain, James T. Kirk. Skippers like Commodore Decker on the *Constellation* and Bob Wesley on the *Lexington* were older men with great accomplishments in their record. But it was the young Captain James T. Kirk who had fired Chekov's imagination.

At thirty-four, Kirk had done more and seen more than Chekov imagined possible. It was Kirk who had helped draw up the Organian Peace Treaty, Kirk again who had gone head-to-head with the Romulans and actually return unscathed.

The *Enterprise* was the first ship to discover the First Federation and to make that critical first contact with the heretofore unknown Gorn, who were near this system. So much adventure. Chekov had been so certain he wanted to be a part of it.

But now there was a nagging doubt in the back of his mind. Was he really up to serving on this ship? He was no longer sure he had what it took to serve under Kirk.

He recalled vividly how, during his first shift on the bridge, he'd nearly navigated the ship in the wrong direction. Sulu had helped cover up the mistake, and the two had become friends, but Chekov kept comparing himself to those other navigators who were paired with the always cheerful lieutenant.

Chekov started when he heard a noise coming from within a collapsed building—but it turned out to be some lab rats scurrying with newfound freedom.

Chekov's thoughts settled again. He sighed. Even when he beamed down as part of a landing party, he never quite felt he was giving it his best. It always seemed to him he could do something more or something better, despite the fact that most of the time the landing parties were surveying lifeless worlds.

It was doubly distressing to know that Captain Kirk was taking note of his every shortcoming. Kirk was his idol, his standard. The man was a living legend, even though he never acted like one—not even the time they were on Beta Damoron V and found themselves in the middle of a revolution.

Trying to measure up to someone of Kirk's stature was a discouraging task at best—one that made him nervous on some occasions and depressed on others. On the other hand, if he was going to become a captain himself one day, he'd *have* to measure up.

All this thinking had Chekov walking blindly, not even listening for warning sounds from the tricorder. He trudged through the debris, glancing now and again at his tricorder for signs of something that might be of value.

At one point he rounded a corner of a burned husk of a building and tripped on a chunk of plastisteel. When he tried to get up, he found himself face-to-face with another corpse.

This time he wasn't sure if it was a man or a woman because the skin had been charred and all traces of hair were gone. The face was a mask of terror, the mouth forever caught in a rictus of a scream. Chekov could almost hear the corpse's voice crying out as death staked its claim.

Breath came raggedly to the Russian as he scrambled to his feet. The sweat that had begun to bead on his forehead now seemed like a torrent; his shirt stuck uncomfortably to his back.

Swallowing hard, Chekov began to walk away from his close encounter. He gulped air a few times, trying to steady himself as he resumed his search.

What brought him back to attention was a resounding crunch. Looking down, Chekov saw a pile of data tapes under his boot. He stopped to look around and realized he was in a research center that had been pretty much leveled. Husks that might have been dead scientists lay under desks or in metal closets.

After bending to wave his tricorder over the debris, Chekov tried to see if any of the data on the tapes could be retrieved. No way, he concluded after a moment or two. He'd destroyed them when he stepped on them. They were now as useless as the computer he'd found earlier. He prepared to redouble his efforts at being vigilant—

He sensed the presence of someone behind him. Whirling, he was startled to see that he was right.

But it was only Captain Kirk, standing there with his hands on his hips, looking none too pleased.

The ensign's hands fumbled with the tricorder, which would have hit the ground had it not been for the safety strap slung over his shoulder. As he quickly scrambled to attention, a fresh torrent of sweat covered his body, and Chekov cringed at what he knew was to come.

"Ensign, have you any idea what just happened?"

"Yes, sir. I accidentally stepped on these computer tapes, ruining the information encoded on them."

Kirk stepped closer to Chekov, narrowing his gaze. The ensign, for his part, actually thought he could feel his pores opening up, letting sweat roll over his body.

"Those tapes may have contained information recorded during the attack."

"Aye, sir. I know, sir."

"In fact, we may have lost a chance to discover who the raiders are . . . thanks to this haphazard approach you have decided to take on a landing-party assignment. Just what are they teaching cadets these days?"

"I don't know, sir."

"No, I suppose you don't. You're not a cadet anymore, mister, and I expect my crewmen to perform better than cadets. Better than any other crew members in the fleet, in fact. Am I making myself clear?"

"Yes, sir. It von't happen again, sir." Chekov felt his accent growing thicker as his brain threatened to freeze up on him.

There was a long pause, and then Kirk seemed to change tactics. "Of course, we don't know what was on those tapes. They may have contained something as useless as fuel-consumption reports.

"But"—and now Kirk began to circle the ensign—"now we'll never know. I dislike not knowing things, Ensign. I do not want any more mistakes on this mission. You understand that?"

"Yes, Keptin. Perfectly."

"Good. Now let's salvage what we can. Dismissed."

Ensign Chekov did as he was told. For the rest of the day he tried not to allow himself to become distracted. When Spock informed him it was time to return to the ship, he glumly joined the rest of the landing party. His last thought before beaming up was an idle one: How did one *avoid* beaming back aboard a starship?

The *Lexington*'s main rec room was a lot like that of the *Enterprise,* not only in appearance but in tone as well. Though the faces were unfamiliar to her, the hum of conversation was easy and subdued, and the occasional riff of laughter sounded hearty and sincere. The only thing that was missing, Uhura told herself, was someone playing a Vulcan harp—or crooning an old African ballad.

Then again, she told herself, it was just as well that the place was relatively quiet. Otherwise she and Baila would have had to sequester themselves someplace stuffy, like the ship's library.

"As I understand it," her fellow communications officer was saying, "the Rithrim have a rather rigid caste system."

"That's right. The population is divided into governors, builders, gatherers, and procreators. There is a strict division of responsibilities."

"Like a Terran insect hive."

She nodded. "Good analogy."

"And we don't know what they want of us?"

Uhura shook her head. "We haven't got a clue."

Baila looked at her, his finely shaped nostrils flaring. "Of course, you're going to find out."

She recognized the remark for the jab it was, but that didn't make it sting any less. *"We're* going to find out," she reminded him. "I will do my part—and you will do yours."

He cocked his head to one side. "Come on, Lieutenant. You're the expert on nonverbal communication. I'm just window dressing, so the Rithrim can see we're taking them seriously."

His voice was calm, smooth. But it didn't disguise the tinge of animosity in his hard, black eyes.

Uhura sighed. "First," she told him, "I am not an expert. I am merely more knowledgeable about nonverbal communication than other available personnel. Second, I'm going to need all the help I can get. Understand?"

"Sure," he replied. "I understand." He looked away from her, as if suddenly interested in something else. "Wouldn't I be an idiot *not* to? I mean, without me, there's no *way* this mission could succeed."

Uhura shook her head. "You know," she said, "you're not making this easy, Mr. Baila." She sat back in her chair. "I've already told you I'm not after your job. What more do you want of me?"

He started to answer, then bit back whatever he was

about to say. Finally he told her: "You're right. This isn't very professional of me. I'm sorry. Whatever problems I've got are my own."

When he met her gaze again, the fire was gone from Baila's eyes. In its place there was a hollowness. Almost a . . . sadness.

Uhura's heart went out to him. Inwardly she cursed herself for being too soft.

In the few moments she'd spent with this man, he'd been either cold or downright insulting. She didn't owe him anything—least of all her pity.

"Look," he said, "maybe we ought to continue this discussion later." He stood. "I'm afraid I'm not very good company right now."

And without another word he left her there in the rec cabin.

A few crewmen looked up to watch Baila go. After the doors had slid closed behind him, they turned to Uhura.

She smiled self-consciously. They smiled back, or shrugged, and then returned to their own conversations.

Uhura bit her lip. This was certainly going to be an *interesting* assignment.

It was some hours later before hunger won out and Chekov left his cabin. He walked to the nearest mess room, hoping not to be seen by too many people along the way. Even though Kirk had dressed down Chekov in private, he was certain word had somehow leaked out. All eyes would be on him.

But when he entered the mess, he was relieved to see just a few people relaxing, finishing meals, or chatting over coffee. He walked over to the food slots and picked up the data tapes with the day's menu. Just holding them made Chekov think of his mistake, and he was tempted to return to his quarters. The rumble from his stomach made him reconsider. Ah, well, better some food than no food at all, he decided.

After carrying his tray to the table, Chekov took the lid off his soup bowl and let the steam soothe him. A whiff of vegetable-beef was all he needed. He grabbed his spoon and attacked the soup eagerly.

"So, how bad was it down there?"

Chekov stopped in mid-slurp, certain he was in trouble again. Looking up, he saw the smiling face of Lieutenant Palmer. She took the seat opposite him and placed her own tray on the table. Company was the one thing he did not desire right then, but the ensign realized he was outranked.

"Bad" was all he felt comfortable saying in reply. He hoped that would be enough. Palmer ate a forkful of her chicken salad and nodded. Chekov debated scalding his mouth in an attempt to rush through his soup and go back to his cabin.

Before he could settle the argument with himself, Palmer looked over and said, "You know, in all my time on the ship, I've never been on a landing party. And here you are, an ensign aboard for just a few months, and you've been to what, six or seven worlds?"

"Four."

"Four. That's four more than me. Not that I'm really complaining, but it would be nice to actually meet some of these people I deal with by communicator. It used to be that way aboard the *Trudeau*. It was a much smaller ship, so we all took turns visiting worlds, even though we never left the Federation."

She paused to eat and Chekov felt obligated to maintain the conversation. Anyone over the rank of ensign held sway over his life, he knew, and at that moment he didn't need any more people thinking ill of him. Captain Kirk was enough.

"So why did you transfer to the *Enterprise?*" he asked, assuming it was a safe enough question.

She finished a bite and patted her lips, her eyes wide. "Why? Same reason most people transfer aboard. This is the ship with the reputation—the Talosians, the Klingons, the Romulans. It's the ship on the cutting edge.

"What I didn't count on was being shipbound. I should've known, though. I don't mind being number two in communications; I mean, Uhura is absolutely inspired. I guess I just want to see a planetary surface other than during a shore leave. You know, I want to do something *exciting.*"

Palmer finished her meal and adjusted a stray blond hair over her ear. "I want to see other races, learn who else is out here. If I'd just wanted to play at communications, I could have stayed at Starfleet Command. No, sir, I want to be a part of the action. Don't you?"

"Yes . . . of course. But don't you worry about making mistakes? Or being blasted by some unknown enemy?" He watched her carefully, checking to see what seasoning did to a crew member's perspective on those basic questions.

"Everyone makes mistakes, Ensign. But we're supposed to learn and prosper by the learning. At least that's what Mr. Spock tells me whenever I screw up.

As for being blasted, I guess it's a risk I'm prepared to take. Of course, serving under Captain Kirk gives one a certain level of security in that regard."

Chekov nodded and thought about her words. She was right, of course, he told himself. Feeling more relaxed about his situation, he finally admitted, "I made a bad mistake today. Worse, Keptin Kirk saw me do it."

"And?"

"And? I considered resigning my commission right then and there. The keptin really rode me. He said he expects the best and I didn't give it."

"So give it next time. Come on. Shift's about to change, and you look as if you need some sleep."

Chekov felt tired, all right. He wasn't surprised that it showed. Standing, he noted that he hadn't finished his meal; maybe he hadn't been as hungry as he thought.

Or maybe it wasn't just food he'd been hungry for. Maybe his conversation with Palmer had given him the energy he needed.

If she could correct her mistakes, so could he. Maybe he could even regain favor with his commanding officer. All he had to do was become the best navigator one could ask for.

But are you up to it? he asked himself. That nagging doubt was still there.

With no ready answer, he accompanied Palmer back to the turbolift and programmed it for the bridge.

Chapter Five

SPOCK LEANED OVER his hooded science station, studying the full spectral analysis the lab was sending up from the debris gathered on Alpha Xaridian II. He sensed, rather than saw, Kirk standing just behind him.

The captain rarely displayed great patience when he was waiting for information.

"Records indicate," Spock said after a moment or two more, "that there is some similarity between the radiation traces left by the raiders' weapons and those produced by the weaponry used by Landorian pirates."

"Landorians?" Kirk frowned at that. "They're a bit far from home."

"Indeed," Spock said. "The concentrated activities of the raiders suggest two possibilities: either they are fairly local, or they are, as humans would put it, 'from out of town—'"

"And they're clustering their activities to make it look as if they're local," said Kirk. "If it's the latter, our job will be that much more difficult. So"—he walked briskly around the perimeter of the bridge to the viewscreen—"let's operate on the presumption and hope that it's the former. Let's check out the neighbors. Put the entire Alpha Xaridian system up on the screen. Let's see who else is in the area."

The viewscreen now displayed a schematic of the entire system—all five planets that constituted the worlds orbiting the star of Alpha Xaridian. Kirk indicated each one, and Spock, using his flawless memory, recounted the specifics.

"Alpha Xaridian One, devoid of life. Alpha Xaridian Two, site of the colony that was attacked. Alpha Xaridian Three, also devoid of life. Alpha Xaridian Four, we believe, was the site of an atomic war a century ago that ripped away the atmosphere and obliterated the populace; no signs of life there. Alpha Xaridian Five is populated and called by its inhabitants Parathu'ul, which means, in their language, Our World."

"Parathu'ul," Kirk said slowly. He continued to stare at it as he said, "We'll run sensor sweeps on One, Three, and Four. If any of the raiders' ships are hiding there, they'll be that much easier to detect." He paused again, then repeated thoughtfully, "Parathu'ul." He tapped it on the screen. "I know that race. They applied for Federation membership, didn't they?"

"That is correct," Spock confirmed. "Three years ago. But it quickly became apparent to all concerned that their prime motive was to obtain certain information about Federation technology that would enable the ruling regime to further its despotic hold on the populace."

"And the Federation refused them membership," said Kirk, "stating that the regime would certainly become even more oppressive if they had access to advanced technology. Hmm. A totalitarian regime with an ax to grind and a hunger for weaponry . . . practically neighbors with a Federation colony that was attacked, and within striking distance of two other beleaguered star systems." And with no warning, he suddenly turned to Chekov. "What does that suggest to you, Mr. Chekov?"

Chekov tried not to act as startled as he was. "That a wisit to the Parath'aa might be in order."

"It might indeed. Set course for Parathu'ul. Let's" —and he sounded almost jaunty—"stop by and say hello, shall we?"

Because the *Enterprise* was proceeding slowly, in order to run sensor scans on the other planets in the Alpha Xaridian system, it was nearly an hour before the starship fell into orbit around Parathu'ul. Within moments after they did so, however, Palmer looked up from the communications board. "We're being hailed by the Parath'aa, Captain," she said.

"Are we, now?" Kirk put on an air of mild surprise. "Imagine that."

"Shall I put them on, sir?"

"Scan the area, Mr. Spock," Kirk said, deferring his reply to Palmer. "Any sign of ships matching the description of the raiders?"

"No sign of any ships in the area aside from ourselves, Captain."

"And on the surface of Parathu'ul? Could the Parath'aa be hiding them?"

"Unlike the *Enterprise*, the raiders have space-to-ground capabilities," said Spock. "In fact, Parathu'ul has a relatively advanced technology, though it is not on par with that of the Federation. Ships could be very easily masked on the planet's surface, and it would be most difficult for our sensors to detect them. Unless, of course, they give off a significant energy discharge, and we happen to be looking in the right place at the time."

"I see." Kirk rubbed his chin thoughtfully.

Palmer spoke up again. "Captain, the Parath'aa are becoming quite insistent."

"Are they? Very well, Lieutenant . . . on screen."

A moment later one of the Parath'aa came on the screen. Inwardly Kirk winced, but his expression never faltered. He had been a starship captain for far too long to let a little thing like aesthetics throw him.

And the Parath'aa were, by human standards, among the least aesthetically pleasing beings in the galaxy. Their skin was so thin as to be nearly translucent, and thus shadows and hints of their inner workings were visible.

The epidermis around their skulls was particularly tightly drawn. Their eyes seemed to float in the sockets, and the Parath'aa looked like a perversely cheerful race, since their teeth seemed set in a permanent grin. The Parath'aa had acquired an under-your-breath nickname in the Federation: the Dead Heads.

"We are hailing the Federation starship in orbit around us," the Parath'aa said formally.

Kirk inclined his head slightly. "This is Captain Kirk, in command of the starship *Enterprise.*"

"You are here about our reapplication to the Federation?" asked the Parath'aa. He sounded almost eager.

Kirk covered his surprise quickly. He'd had no idea that the Parath'aa were once again lobbying the Federation for membership. This, however, could quickly be turned to his advantage. "We are exploring the possibility, yes," said Kirk neutrally.

"You are coming then to surface of Parathu'ul?"

"If that is acceptable," Kirk said.

"We are in expectation of you, then," said the Parath'aa. "I am being planetary head Silva."

"We are being on our way, Silva," Kirk told him. *"Enterprise* out." He stood as the rather difficult image of the Parath'aa blinked off the screen. "Mr. Spock, ready the transporter room to beam a landing party to the surface: myself, Dr. McCoy, Mr. Sulu, and Mr. Giotto."

"I am to continue sensor sweeps of the planet to see if there is any evidence of the raiding ships," said Spock.

"Mr. Spock, you read my mind."

The landing party arrived on Parathu'ul a few minutes later, materializing in the center of Silva's office. Several other Parath'aa were standing in a small semicircle, and Silva introduced each one of them in turn. Their names were virtually unpronounceable, and Kirk suspected that Silva's real name was, as well. Probably he had used a more human-sounding equivalent for the convenience of the *Enterprise* captain and crew. It was a rather considerate gesture for Silva to make.

And another considerate, or at least somewhat fortunate, aspect was that the Parath'aa disliked being touched. Instead, they bowed slightly from the hip, or the equivalent of the hip. Their bodies were oddly structured; their waists seemed to be situated just under the human equivalent of the armpits.

"Captain Kirk," said Silva softly, "you honor us with your presence. And you surprise us, I must admit. It was only several days ago that we sent our transmission to the UFP regarding our reapplication for admittance. That you would arrive so quickly . . . I am impressed."

"We happened to be in the area," said Kirk. "Think of it as one of those serendipitous things."

"You are being also fortunate to catch us on a pleasant day," he said. "Weather on Parathu'ul is notoriously unpleasant, yet here . . . look. The sun is shining," and he gestured to the window of his office. "You are bringing good climates with you, Captain. A good omen."

Kirk glanced out the window, and the view was extremely pleasant. The buildings of the capital city were tall, gleaming spires. The streets looked extremely clean. There was a good deal of bustling about on the main avenue below, but the crowd was orderly and well mannered.

"Matters have improved on Parathu'ul since our previous UFP contact," Silva continued. "Our population is being much more content. Vastly improved mass transit has improved the quality of life. Peoples are happier, wealthier than they have ever been. The air is being cleared. Unlike the previous regime, we are being more lenient with those who speak their mind. We are being"—he paused, searching for the right term, and then his face brightened—"vacation spot."

"Vacation spot?" Kirk smiled lopsidedly at that. He looked at the other members of the landing party for confirmation as he said, "Well . . . that would hardly seem likely, what with the problem with the raiders."

"Raiders?" Silva seemed genuinely puzzled.

"The raiders who attacked Alpha Xaridian Two," Sulu now spoke up. "Certainly you were aware of it?"

Silva frowned, and one of his advisers leaned over and whispered in his ear—or at least the equivalent of his ear. Silva's temples visibly throbbed. "Oh! Of course. Yes, the unpleasantness of a short time ago. That is being very unfortunate." He shook his head. "Very unfortunate."

"It appears," McCoy said, "that you were lucky enough to be spared."

"You've had no contact with the raiders at all?" Giotto asked.

"None," said Silva. "We agree, yes, we are being lucky. It would seem that the luck of the Parath'aa is changing, yes? Only short years ago, UFP wishes to

75

have nothing to do with us. And now be looking at us. Healthy, prosperous. No trouble with raiders, with—"

There was a noise from the street below. Kirk frowned. "What's that?"

"What is being what?" asked Silva. His mouth was drawn back in that typical rictus smile.

"That shouting, from the crowd."

Kirk went to the window and looked down.

Approaching the front of the building was a small band of protesters. They were carrying placards, waving signs and shaking their fists in anger. It was clear that they were unhappy about something. He turned to Silva. "What's the problem there?"

"Have-nots," said Silva.

Kirk and the others exchanged a glance. "Have-nots?" asked Sulu.

Silva patted himself on the chest and indicated the others as well. "Haves." He pointed out to the street, toward the protesters. "Have-nots. Always are being, yes? Always being case. Always are being small, small minority who are unhappy about being have-nots. But it will not be spoiling lovely day, yes?"

Now there were the sounds of scuffling, and the noises of protest were abruptly drowned out by the sounds of weapons fire. The *Enterprise* team looked down at the street in horror as, before their eyes, the Parath'aa who had been leading the protest were cut down at close range. The deadly and efficient Parath'aat blasters were being wielded by what appeared to be armed security guards who did their job very efficiently and very brutally.

Bodies were cleaved clean in half, upper sections

falling away from the lower, heads being severed at the neck. Others in the crowd who had been shouting agreement with the protesters now quickly faded into the safety of the mob, getting as far from the scene of the slaughter as quickly as they could.

Kirk turned toward Silva and made no attempt to hide his anger and disgust. He pointed a shaking finger toward the window in disgust as he said, "You support that . . . that *hideous* display of oppression . . . and you still claim that you're being more tolerant of those who speak out against you!"

"Not tolerant." Silva corrected him politely. "Lenient. Our predecessors would arrest protesters and then torture them publicly before killing them. We are being"—he mimed a throat-cutting gesture—"merciful. We are being lenient, yes? Those who are being publicly unhappy, openly protesting—they are knowing there will be no torture. Instead, quick death. Improvement, yes?" He looked from one man to the other with almost puppy-dog eagerness.

McCoy could barely get a word out, and when he did, he whispered it, sarcastically: "Vast."

Kirk's communicator beeped, and he flipped it open. He tried to keep his voice neutral. "Kirk here."

"Captain," came Spock's voice, "the survey we discussed is completed. Possibilities of camouflage still exist, but at present there is no sign."

"Thank you, Mr. Spock. Prepare to beam us up."

"Is there being problem?"

"No problem, Silva," Kirk assured him. "None at all."

"You are being recommending of us, then? Tell UFP of our softening of our stance?"

"I'm sure they'll be interested to hear every detail," Kirk said.

"About cleanliness and better life here on Parathu'ul?"

"Absolutely."

"Mass transit. Tell them we are having trains running on time."

Kirk looked at him askance. "Somehow, Silva, I don't doubt that. Mr. Spock, four to beam up."

Moments later the landing party vanished in the shimmer of the *Enterprise* transporter beams. Silva turned and grinned the perpetual Parath'aa grin at his associates.

"We are being in for certain," he said.

Chapter Six

DOWN IN ENGINEERING, lights flickered on the portable scanner being waved over a vast collection of junk—all of it remnants of the Alpha Xaridian II colony. Frowning over the readouts, Scott tried adjusting the scanner. There was no change in the readings—a result that did not improve the engineer's mood.

"I canna understand why someone would want to destroy a colony," he muttered. Scott's hand went out for his coffee cup, and he absently raised it to his lips. Cold. It figured. Replacing it on the table, he returned his gaze to the scanner.

While Scott enjoyed ripping mechanical things apart, he hated seeing someone do it for no apparent reason. Like the captain, Scott hated mysteries. He wanted to understand what had happened in the Xaridian systems, which was why he'd personally taken over the inspection of the material that had been beamed up from the ruined colony.

Another reason, he had to admit, if only to himself, was that with the ship just moving through space, things were too normal, too close to the edge of suspense for him. Instead of pacing back and forth in his engine room, which he knew like the back of his hand, Scott preferred studying the debris.

Of course the investigative teams from the science division had gone through the material under Spock's scrupulous supervision. But they had agreed that Scott might have a different point of view. At his request, some members of the landing party were assisting him—including Ensign Chekov, who was taking measurements of some charred, melted equipment with a tricorder.

Snapping off his sensor, Scott looked about him and sighed. He had been going after this for two hours and seemed no closer to a clue than before. He thought maybe some walking about would clear the mind.

Scott stretched and began pacing the room, watching the others at work. He stopped at the food dispenser and summoned another cup of hot coffee. Sipping at it carefully, he continued to watch the others. He noted that Chekov was readjusting his tricorder, so he walked over to observe.

Chekov and Scott had not worked much together, but the engineer considered him a fine young man.

"Something, laddie?" Scott stepped closer as Chekov finished adjusting the tricorder.

Chekov looked up briefly and then returned his gaze to the screen. "Maybe, Mr. Scott. I am trying to boost the lower-range readings. I think we may have something new."

"Aye. Try using the Feinberger attachment for more detailed readings," Scott suggested.

Chekov opened a small hatch on the front of the tricorder, and out popped a small circular device, which was electronically connected to the main tricorder. While medical science teams used the devices more than any other crew members, the Feinberger scanners had a multitude of uses. Waving the small, twinkling device within an inch of the machinery, Chekov looked carefully at the tiny readout screen.

"Ah, I think I have something. The spikes on the lowest electromagnetic column may be an energy signature. Maybe Mr. Spock can extrapolate from this and find out just how powerful these cossacks really are."

Scotty looked at Chekov's tricorder and took a cautious sip of his coffee. He thought for a moment and then looked again at the tricorder.

"I don't think so," he said, taking the Feinberger from the surprised ensign. Scotty waved it in front of the slagged metal and then looked at the tricorder for confirmation of his suspicion.

"What you found here is a signature, all right—but it's nae from the weaponry. It's residue from the equipment's own power supply. See how it follows a very standard pulse pattern? It's the same on dozens of different machines. Sorry, laddie, but you've found nothing new yet." Scott reached out and tried to put a reassuring hand on Chekov's shoulder, but he felt the younger man tense.

"Damn!" the ensign exploded through clenched teeth. The vehemence of his tone took Scott by surprise. "When am I going to get something right? I follow the book, I do as I'm told, and I keep getting it wrong! Tell me, Mr. Scott, is there some reason I'm *always* wrong?" The pained look on the ensign's face caused Scott some serious concern, and he tried to defuse the young man's anger.

"Ye're an ensign, laddie. Haven't ye learned by now that ensigns are never right?" He grinned. "I dinna do any better when I first shipped out. Look at it this way: if ye start off perfect, you've got a very dull life ahead of ye."

Chekov shook his head and sighed loudly. "I've done what I can here. I'll log my report—vhat little I have to tell—and return to the bridge," he said in a monotone. Standing, he snapped shut his tricorder and restored it to the cubby near the door.

"Laddie, I could use a hand with this larger piece," Scotty said quietly. While he had been reviewing it for hours already, Scott thought he could at least try to diffuse the ensign's frustration with work—even though it might double the frustration the chief engineer felt himself.

Hefting the larger engineering scanner, with its triangular design, the engineer aimed it directly at the center of the molten metal. Chekov slowly walked over to Scott's side and watched.

"Here now," the engineer said, gesturing to the remnant. "I'm tryin' the opposite of what you just did. We'll go to the upper end of the spectrum, with a more powerful diagnostic tool. Check my readouts, would ye?"

All right, so maybe it was make-work, but long ago Scott had learned that if people were to keep performing and learning, they had to stay busy. Too much time with their thoughts and they sooner or later couldn't figure out how to turn on their computer.

Using Scott's own tricorder, Chekov matched readings with the larger device. Scott slowly moved the scanner over every millimeter of the metal. Narrowing his eyes, Chekov appeared to be absorbed in the activity—looking for something, anything.

For what seemed like a long time there was nothing out of the ordinary. The scan bars on Chekov's tricorder remained flat and steady.

Suddenly there was a color jump into the blue portion of the spectrum and then a powerful spike downward. Scott watched Chekov blink and moved the tricorder closer to his own eyes. Another blue shift and then a deeper spike downward. The pattern was repeated with the downward motions remaining at a constant depth.

"Meester Scott, you found something!" Chekov exclaimed.

"Aye? What is it, lad?"

"I do not know . . . yet. But it is definitely showing as a radiation reading—and it is not anything the tricorder recognizes."

"Now, that's something. Let's have a look," Scott said, and held out his hand. He read the tricorder screen more closely, relieved that Chekov had accomplished something worthwhile. Of course he should have thought of checking the upper register earlier, but that was water under the bridge; this was definitely something to study further.

He resolved not to forget to mention Chekov's contribution when he made his report. Anything to help the young man, Scott figured. He recalled that it was not that long ago he was a junior engineer on the *Enterprise* under Captain Christopher Pike, and there had been many frustrating moments when he thought his skills were less than a match for the expectations of his superior officers.

"Thanks for the assistance, laddie. Now off with ye, while I finish this up. The briefing is to start in a little while and I've got t' have this report ready."

Chekov looked up suddenly. "I did not know of any briefing."

Scott coughed to cover his surprise. He should have realized Kirk was going to keep Chekov in the dark until the ensign regained the captain's confidence. "It's for senior officers," he managed to get out.

"That usually means bridge staff. That usually means . . . me," Chekov stammered. He slumped his shoulders and left the room.

Scott watched with sympathetic eyes. I'll have to talk with that boy, he thought. But first, we have this problem to deal with.

As Rithra came up on the main viewscreen, it became obvious to Uhura that it was a class-M world. It was somewhat bigger than Earth, but its gravity, atmosphere, and meteorological characteristics were well within the limits of human tolerance.

Of course, class-M status didn't necessarily mean a world would be aesthetically pleasing when seen from space. As it happened, this one was positively breathtaking in its cloud-wreathed umber-and-aquamarine majesty. And from her vantage point beside the commodore's command chair, Uhura certainly had the time to appreciate the view.

"Approaching the planet," announced Berriman, Wesley's pretty redheaded helmsman.

"Slow to half-impulse," the commodore told her. "Prepare to enter orbit, Mr. Ito."

"Aye, sir," responded Ito, the stocky, dark-eyed navigator. "All preparations in place."

Wesley's orders were phrased a little differently—perhaps stronger in tone—from the ones issued by Captain Kirk, Uhura noted. But then, Kirk and the commodore were different people. And anyway, it was the results that really counted.

"Open hailing frequencies," Wesley said.

"Hailing frequencies open," Baila confirmed.

Uhura experienced a twinge; it felt strange to hear someone else say those words. She couldn't help but glance back at the communications station, where Baila was running through the required protocols. With a small sigh, she turned back to the screen.

"Something wrong, Lieutenant?" Wesley looked up at her, expecting an answer.

Uhura clasped her hands behind her back as she turned back to the viewscreen. "No, sir. It's just that I'm not used to . . . well . . ."

"Approaching a planet without having to open hailing frequencies?"

She shrugged. "Something like that."

Turning back to the main viewscreen, Wesley chuckled. "Nothing like a new perspective to make

you remember why you signed up in the first place—
eh, Lieutenant?"

Uhura returned his gaze and finally nodded. "I
suppose so, sir."

For a moment the commodore continued to study
her. Then Baila spoke up.

"I have a response from the Rithrim," he reported.

Straightening in his seat, Wesley addressed the
viewer. "On screen, Mr. Baila."

A fraction of a second later the image of a
Rithramen governor appeared—though it was difficult to make out at first, given the amount of ambient
illumination that accompanied it. Uhura had to
squint to compensate, though the brightness didn't
surprise her; she'd learned about the Rithrim's love of
light in her studies.

As her eyes adjusted, she was able to see more of the
governor. Like all Rithrim, he was basically
humanoid, with pinkish orange skin, small black eyes,
and a feathery crest on his head. Though the
viewscreen showed only his head and shoulders,
Uhura knew that his body was tall and slender—a
trait peculiar to the governor caste.

"Welcome," said the Rithrim. "I am Endris,
present-cycle governor of Rithra." As he spoke, his
hands danced quickly but gracefully.

Uhura frowned, trying to keep up. She hadn't
expected the Rithrim's hand language to proceed at
such a breakneck speed.

"Lieutenant?" Wesley breathed without looking up
at her.

"He's embellishing the greeting," she explained,

though some of the details had eluded her. "You're not just welcome, you're *very* welcome."

The commodore smiled. "I'm very pleased to have such a gracious host," he told the governor.

Uhura made the necessary signs for emphasis, so Wesley's remark would be overlaid with the same enthusiasm as the Rithrim's.

"I see," observed the governor, "that you have brought along an interpreter."

The commodore nodded. "As you know, our translation devices do not supply us with the complete meaning of your communications. Lieutenant Uhura is familiar enough with your gestures to give us the information we lack."

The Rithrim eyed Uhura for a moment. He said nothing, but his hands pantomimed approval of her.

"If you would like to beam down now," Endris suggested, "we can supply the necessary coordinates." Again his remarks were accompanied by a series of quick, deft signals.

The more she saw of the governor's hand language, the easier it was for Uhura to follow. "Interesting," she said, low enough so only Wesley could hear it. "He seems impatient. There's a definite note of urgency in his gestures."

"Any idea why?" asked the commodore, also speaking sotto voce.

"None," she told him.

Wesley grunted softly. "We would be happy to beam down now," he informed the Rithrim, raising his voice again. Uhura reinforced his statement, to make it clear he had no reservations whatsoever.

"Receiving those coordinates, sir," Baila reported from the communications station. "And relaying them to the transporter room."

As if that were the cue he'd been waiting for, the governor inclined his feather-crested head. A moment later his image vanished from the screen, to be replaced by the regal aspect of Rithra.

"Thank you, Mr. Baila," said Wesley. He stood and turned to Uhura. "Let's see what that urgency's about, shall we?"

"Let's," she agreed.

The commodore cast a sweeping glance over his bridge. "Berriman, you've got the conn. Samuels and Baila, you're with me." Before the words were entirely out of his mouth, he was on his way to the turbolift.

As Uhura materialized with the others, she was glad for the precautions Dr. Coss had insisted they all take to protect their eyes. Even with her polarized visor, which curved around the top half of her face, she found the ambient light too bright for comfort. The viewscreen, with its automatic compensating filters, had only hinted at the intensity of this world's natural illumination.

Looking around to get her bearings, she found herself in a large, ancient-looking courtyard constructed of a material that looked very much like sandstone. An abundance of frescoed walls, carved corner pillars, and freestanding statuary made of the same material as the basic structure gave the place a feeling of vigor and enthusiasm—of teeming, joyful energies yearning for application.

The focal point of the courtyard was a small pool, a

perfect square of still water that reflected the vibrant blue-green sky overhead. On either side of the pool was a bench. And one of the benches was occupied by five tall figures wearing black robes.

"The governors' council," someone whispered— Uhura wasn't sure who. She was too busy watching the nearest robed figure as he rose and gestured to the bench on the opposite side of the pool.

The lieutenant recognized him as the present-cycle governor, Endris. "Please," he said. "Sit."

"I don't think we need a translation for *that,*" commented Wesley.

As one, Uhura and the others crossed to the proferred bench. Only after his guests had made themselves comfortable did Endris himself sit down.

For a moment each group surveyed the other, careful not to actually stare. Beside Uhura, the commodore cleared his throat.

"It is our understanding," he began, "that the matter which brought us here is an urgent one. If it's all the same to you, we'd like to dispense with protocol and hear how we can help."

A little blunt, Uhura reflected, as she used her hand gestures to soften Wesley's opening just a bit. But then, as she was learning, the commodore wasn't one to mince words.

Some of the governors exchanged glances, though Endris continued to regard Wesley and his party. "We appreciate your candor," the Rithrim said. There was no trace of irony or resentment in his hand motions.

As Uhura waited for more, she saw movement at the far end of the courtyard. Squinting, she picked out three figures—Rithrim, like the governors, but squatter and more powerful-looking. Also, they were dressed in more functional outfits. And they were carrying some sort of tools.

Builders, she guessed. That would explain the physical discrepancies: they were of a different caste than Endris and his companions.

Glancing at the Federation personnel but passing no comments, the newcomers moved unobtrusively to a corner of the yard. After putting their tools down on the ground, they seemed to inspect a portion of the carvings—a portion that, now that Uhura took a closer look, appeared to be in need of repair.

Then she had to forget about them for a while. Endris was speaking again.

"It is in the spirit of that candor," he went on, "that I will tell you this: there is a place called Girin Gatha, not more than a few hundred kilometers south of here. It is the site of an important Rithramen facility —and it is threatened by an active heat."

Uhura felt her companions turning to her. "A *heat?*" asked Samuels.

"Obviously a word that has many different meanings in this culture," noted Baila. "The nonverbal modifier will determine its specific meaning here."

Ignoring the exchange, Uhura focused on the governor's hand signals—but failed to catch their meaning. Apparently understanding her difficulty, Endris repeated himself.

"Ah," she said. "I get it now. A heat, in this case, is a volcano."

"Lousy planning," muttered Coss, "to put an important facility next to a volcano."

The commodore shot him a discouraging look, then

turned again to the governor. "If I may ask, what's the problem? A force-shield should protect your facility from a . . . a heat." He waited for Uhura to differentiate the word from its various other meanings. "And our data on Rithra indicate that you developed shield technology some time ago."

"That is correct," Endris agreed. "What is more, we have successfully employed this technology at Girin Gatha for many years. However, the molten minerals produced by the heat in recent months have been marked by a certain amount of radioactivity."

"So that's it," said Samuels. "The radiation is playing havoc with shield integrity. I've seen that sort of thing before."

The governor signed his agreement. "Our shields are failing to hold back the molten flow. And though it advances slowly, it may be only a matter of weeks before our facility is destroyed." He paused. "The Federation's shield technology is more advanced than ours. It is our hope that you will be able to construct a shield generator at Girin Gatha that will render the facility secure again."

The governor—indeed, all the governors—seemed calm as this information was dispensed. However, judging by their hand movements, there was a terrific emotional charge behind that calm. Uhura reported as much to her commanding officer.

"I see," said Wesley. Then, to Samuels: "How long will it take to rig up a shield generator for these people?"

The first officer shrugged. "Depends on the size of the area being shielded, the terrain, and the nature of the lava flow, of course—its volume, its speed, things like that. But I'd be surprised if we couldn't do it in a few days. Maybe less, if we really pushed ourselves."

Wesley turned to the Rithrim. "How's that sound?" Again Uhura softened the edges of his question with a series of polite, graceful gestures.

Endris signed his exhilaration. "It sounds most pleasing," he answered. "Most pleasing indeed."

"Good," said the commodore. "I have to warn you, though—I don't know about *your* shield generators, but ours have been known to go down from time to time. If I were you, I'd plan on relocating the facility to a safer place."

"We cannot," replied Endris. His hands moved more quickly, more forcefully, to underscore his inflexibility on that point.

"Why not?" asked Samuels.

Again the council members exchanged glances. And again the present-cycle governor remained steadfast in his attention to the visitors.

"You see," said Endris, his hands proceeding slowly again, "the facility is one of our major reproductive centers. It is used by our procreator caste to produce new generations of Rithrim. And procreators can perform their function only in the place where they were born."

"That's right," said Coss. "I remember reading about that. The Rithrim are like salmon back on Earth—they have to return to their birthplace to spawn."

Samuels grunted. "What a complimentary analogy, Doctor."

Wesley regarded the benchful of governors. "That answers my question," he assured them.

Endris signed his satisfaction that the commodore had been accommodated. And there was a pause as Wesley prepared to broach the second topic they'd come to discuss with the Rithrim.

Uhura took advantage of the respite to observe the builders again. They were continuing their inspection of the carvings, running their fingers over them and communicating with one another by means of gestures alone.

As she watched, they seemed to reach a conclusion. One of them picked up a tool and, as quietly as possible, began to chip away at one of the carvings under consideration. No doubt, the lieutenant mused, a preliminary to repair.

Then her attention was drawn back to the commodore, who'd finally decided on the right approach. "There is another matter," he told Endris and the others, "which is unrelated to the one we've already discussed. And that is the Federation's desire to establish an observatory here on Rithra. I take it you've had time to digest the detailed plans we sent you?"

Uhura used her hands to emphasize the word "unrelated," making it plain that this was not a quid pro quo situation. In other words, it wasn't necessary for the Rithrim to allow the observatory in order to obtain help in protecting their procreation center.

When both Wesley and Uhura were done, Endris replied. "We have indeed had the opportunity to review your plans. And we see no reason for work on the observatory not to begin as soon as possible."

Like Uhura's gestures a moment earlier, the present-cycle governor's made it clear that the obser-

THE DISINHERITED

vatory issue was separate from that of the procreation center. She couldn't help but smile. Apparently the Rithrim had decided to allow the Federation its facility regardless of what else transpired.

During her tenure on the *Enterprise,* Uhura had seen a number of negotiations start out promisingly and end in frustration or failure. It was nice to see this one going so well.

"Thank you," said the commodore. "We appreciate that. And I'd like to pursue the matter further—*after* we secure the procreation center." Then, looking at his fellow officers, he added: "Unless anyone else has something to contribute, I suggest we get back to the ship and organize an engineering team."

Uhura had contributed all she could; apparently, so had everyone else. When the commodore stood, they all followed suit. A moment later the Rithrim stood as well.

"We are indebted to you for your assistance in this matter," said Endris.

"Think nothing of it," replied Wesley. Uhura made sure to soften the edges of that remark, too.

The commodore took out his communicator and snapped off a command: "Beam us up, Lieutenant."

"Aye, sir," came the response.

It took a couple of seconds before they started to dematerialize. As she waited, Uhura was able to concentrate a little more on the builders at the far end of the courtyard.

They were all chipping away now, though their actions were still confined to a small area. Momentarily she had a funny feeling—that they weren't repairing the carving, but obliterating it.

But that's silly, she told herself. Why would anyone want to destroy an ancient carving? Perhaps it had seen better days, but it certainly didn't present a danger to anyone.

Then the transporter effect claimed her and she found herself back on the *Lexington*.

"You've been very fortunate, Miss Jarvis," Kirk said.

Sharon Jarvis, the colony administrator of Beta Xaridian IV, nodded in agreement with the captain's assessment.

They were walking down the center street of the colony. Kirk thought there was nothing particularly impressive about the settlement—unlike the more elaborate colony in the neighboring Alpha Xaridian star system, this outpost on Beta Xaridian IV seemed almost rough-and-tumble. The colonists that Kirk noticed going about their business were more of a mix than the largely human population of Alpha Xaridian II. The colonists of Beta Xaridian IV seemed grittier, tougher . . . and also, it seemed, at least two-thirds of them were female.

Administrator Jarvis was typical of the population. She was not a particularly tall woman; she was a bit stocky, solidly built, and muscular, with short hair shot through with gray.

Montgomery Scott approached them, accompanied by Giotto. Scotty was absentmindedly wiping his hands on his uniform legs, as if to rid himself of some grease that he might have acquired. That wouldn't have surprised Kirk in the least. Scotty had a tendency to get right into the thick of things—behavior far better suited to lower echelon engineering personnel than to the chief engineer. But Kirk was certainly not going to be the one to tell Scotty to change the way he did things.

"Planetary defense systems check out, Captain," Scotty said approvingly.

"I could have told you that," said Jarvis, taking a drag on her cheroot. "My people are the best—no insult intended to your own, of course."

"None taken, Miss Jarvis," said Kirk. "There's room in the galaxy for several 'bests,' I've always thought."

"Captain," Giotto spoke up, "it might not be a bad idea to evacuate the colonists."

Jarvis looked at Giotto in surprise. "Now why in hell should we be evacuated?"

"As the captain said," Giotto observed, "you've been lucky. The raiders who have been savaging colony worlds in the Xaridian systems have, thus far, not attacked you. Perhaps it would be best for you to leave before there is some sort of unpleasantness."

Jarvis looked him up and down, then turned to Kirk. "Do you concur with this opinion, Captain?"

Kirk pursed his lips. "Over on Alpha Xaridian Two, we came in in the middle of a fairly heated discussion on that very topic. The colony had been ravaged, and the population was debating as to whether they should leave or not."

"What did you tell them?"

Kirk cleared his throat. "I . . . told them they were brave individuals facing a galaxy filled with danger."

"And they stayed."

"They stayed, yes," Kirk said. "But so far the

raiders have not attacked any given world more than once. Relatively speaking, those colonists are safe where they are. You, on the other hand, remain a viable target . . . and judging from the destruction over in Gamma Xaridian, the raiders are getting more, not less, vicious. Perhaps it might make more sense for you to—"

"Run like hell?" she asked, her eyes twinkling slightly. "Captain, this wouldn't have anything to do with the fact that this colony is run by, and has a high population of, females, would it? Making you feel a bit more protective?"

"Certainly not, Miss Jarvis," Kirk said, bristling slightly more than he needed to.

"Because if you were, I'd understand it. I think it would show a rather charming streak of chivalry in you."

"In that case"—Kirk allowed a small smile— "there might be some protectiveness at work here."

"That's what I thought," said Jarvis. "You men are all alike. This is the twenty-third century, and you still figure that we women need your strong arms to protect us."

Kirk was taken aback. "Wait a minute. You said you thought chivalry was charming."

"I lied."

He stared at her for a moment and then laughed. After only a moment's hesitation, she joined him.

"Miss Jarvis, I believe you when you say you can take care of yourselves. Still . . . considering the track record of these raiders, I think my concern can be chalked up to something other than misplaced chivalry."

"Understood, Captain," replied Jarvis. "But the bottom line is, my people and I are not going to be scared off."

"Perhaps that's the intention of the raiders," Kirk admitted. "To try to get everyone off the colony planets. And fear is just as effective a weapon as anything else."

"More efficient, too," commented Scotty. "You dinna have to worry about casualties or expending energy."

"But why do they want us to leave?" said Jarvis. "Even if the reason for the attacks is to get people off the worlds . . . that can't be the sole motive. There must be some further incentive. Territorial gain, maybe. Or maybe there's something on the planets that they want."

"We're exploring all the possibilities, Miss Jarvis, I can assure you of th—"

The communicator beeped, and Kirk quickly answered.

"Captain," came Palmer's voice, "we're receiving a distress call from Gamma Xaridian Eight."

"Another planet in the Gamma system," said Kirk grimly. "The raiders?"

"It would appear so, sir."

"Beam us up immediately. I want the helm ready with warp speed the second my foot hits the transporter pad. Kirk out."

Scotty and Giotto stepped closer to Kirk as Jarvis stepped back. "God watch over you, Captain," she said.

"If He will," said Kirk. "And the same goes for you."

"If She will," replied Jarvis, and she noted Kirk's small smile as the *Enterprise* officers beamed away.

Please don't let me screw up.

Chekov was certain that his hands were trembling as he laid in the course that would take them, via the most direct possible route, to the beleaguered Gamma Xaridian VIII. He was dimly aware of Sulu's eyes on him as he worked, but said nothing. He performed a last-minute check on his calculations just before he entered them into the computer, but then his hand stopped in midair above his instruments. Something was not right. He was overlooking some detail. And then he realized what it was even as Sulu said in a low, amused voice, "So you noticed it, huh?"

He turned to Sulu, feeling the blood drain from his cheeks as he said, "I was about to make the correction."

"Good," Sulu said affably. "Following a course straight through the Gamma Xaridian sun might not have left us in very good shape to stop the raiders once we got there."

The turbolift door hissed open, and Kirk entered quickly. Spock rose from the command chair as Kirk took his place. "Take us out of orbit, Mr. Sulu."

"Aye, sir."

"Course plotted and laid in, Keptin," said Chekov. He glanced at Sulu, but the helmsman was busy and didn't spare the young ensign so much as a glance.

"ETA at warp seven, Mr. Sulu?"

"Twenty-two minutes, Captain."

"Let's hope to God it's fast enough. Warp seven, helm. Take us out of here."

The *Enterprise* whipped out of orbit and launched itself into warp space the moment it was clear of the planet's atmosphere.

The blare of the red alert signal sounded everywhere, but it was loudest in Chekov's head. There was room in it only for the noise and for the recurring thought that was almost a mantra: *Please don't let me screw up.*

Chapter Seven

LIKE THE REST OF the Federation team, Uhura had been briefed by the Rithramen builders whom Endris had put in touch with them. But no amount of briefing could have prepared her for what she saw when she beamed down.

To the west, a volcano of staggering proportions was discharging a steady tide of lurid liquid rock. The tide was deflected by the invisible barrier of the Rithrim's shields some fifty meters beyond the facility, but that didn't make it any less frightening.

To the north and south the deflected lava crawled along the shields and flowed into the blinding expanse of blue-green sea that surrounded the procreation center on three sides. Where cool water and red-hot rock collided along the shore, massive sizzling clouds of steam rose up to fatten the clouds overhead.

The facility itself was simple and boxlike—perhaps fifty meters by fifty meters and two stories high. Though it was apparently constructed of the same kind of stone as the governors' courtyard, the place was much more stark and modern-looking, like the statuary surrounding it, which celebrated all four Rithramen castes.

"Damn," breathed Wesley, who'd accompanied Uhura. He adjusted his visor. "Ever see a place quite like this one, Lieutenant?"

"Can't say I have," Uhura muttered, taking a few steps toward the shield.

She watched the lava roil against it. It was like a struggle between force and restraint, between order and chaos. And a small Rithramen building where babies were conceived and nurtured stood amid this clash of elemental powers—and survived.

It was remarkable. It was *more* than remarkable.

"Welcome to Girin Gatha," called a robust and familiar voice. Turning, Uhura saw Samuels trekking across the humpbacked sweep of sandy rock that fronted the facility. The first officer had been down here for nearly an hour, helping the *Lexington*'s engineering people survey the terrain.

He wiped his brow as he approached; his tunic was marred by dark sweat stains. "Nice place to visit," Samuels remarked, "but I wouldn't want to have to procreate here."

Uhura smiled. "Good thing you don't have to," she told him.

The man was beginning to grow on her, she decided. Even if you didn't like his sense of humor, it was hard to argue with his dedication; no officer she had seen worked harder than Wynn Samuels.

Turning to the commodore, he asked, "What brings you down here, sir?"

Wesley shrugged. "The lieutenant here thought it might be a good idea for us to see the place." He cast Uhura a sidewise glance. "If the subject comes up again, she says, we'll be better off knowing what we're talking about." A pause. "And after a moment's reflection I had to agree with her. So here we are."

"I see," said the first officer. "In that case, you might want to do your observing from inside the building. It's a lot more comfortable in there." He swept a lock of sweat-matted hair out of his eyes. "Just because I'm nutty enough to be out here doesn't mean you have to be nutty too."

Wesley looked at Uhura. He indicated the procreation center with a tilt of his head. "Shall we?" he asked.

Uhura hesitated. "With all due respect," she said finally, "I'm not that eager for comfort, Commodore. I don't mind a little perspiration if it means being able to see something I've never seen before. I mean, isn't that the reason we signed up in the first place?"

Wesley regarded her, remembering where he'd heard the words before, and from whom. Slowly, a smile spread across his face. "Right you are, Lieutenant. And thanks for reminding me." He turned to Samuels. "You see?" he said. "Now *that's* a communications officer."

The first officer cleared his throat, obviously feeling awkward about participating in any implied swipe at Baila—particularly in front of one of Baila's peers.

"I'd best be getting back to the engineering team," he said. And with a nod that was meant for both of them, he turned and made his way back across the humpbacked front yard of the building.

As he vanished from sight, the commodore regarded Uhura. "I didn't mean that to sound like an indictment of Mr. Baila, Lieutenant—even though it came out that way."

"It's all right, Commodore. I understand."

Wesley frowned. He seemed to be thinking about something. Finally he said: "Can I ask you something off the record, Lieutenant?"

That caught her a little off-balance, but she nodded. "Sure."

The commodore's frown deepened; he actually looked angry. "You've spoken with Baila a few times now—and you're obviously a perceptive woman. Can you tell me what's made him stop caring?"

Uhura didn't know quite what to say to that. "Stop caring?" she echoed.

Wesley held up his hands. "Listen, if I'm intruding on a confidence, or if you just plain feel uncomfortable talking about a colleague, I'll back off. It's just that he used to be a good officer—a very good officer. And now he's something less than that."

The communications officer swallowed. So Baila wasn't far off the mark at all. His job *was* in jeopardy.

Unfortunately Uhura couldn't answer Wesley's question. She said so.

The commodore accepted her response. "Just thought I'd give it a shot," he told her. "No harm in trying, eh?"

"No, sir. No harm in that."

Wesley rubbed his hands together. "Well then, we came down here to look around. Let's look around, for God's sake. Any idea where you'd like to start?"

Uhura scanned the area. "Well," she said, "we've seen the volcano side. Why not take a look around back?"

"Sounds good to me," he agreed.

As they walked in that direction, the hissing produced by the meeting of lava and seawater grew louder. By the time they reached the space between the procreation center and the sea, the sound was almost deafening, though the droplets of water in the air offered them some relief from the heat.

For a while the sputtering clash of molten rock and lapping tide mesmerized Uhura. Then she turned to the commodore and saw that he wasn't looking at the shoreline anymore.

He was staring back at the building itself. And as she followed his gaze, she saw what had caught his eye.

There were several gaps in the ring of statuary around the back of the procreation center—places with pedestals but no figures. It was as if someone had vandalized the grounds, cutting down the statues at their ankles. And yet, all their intelligence on the Rithrim indicated that there was no crime on this world.

Wesley grunted. "What do you suppose happened there?" he asked. "Those statues don't look old enough to need replacement."

At first the communications officer was at a loss. Then she remembered the builders back in the courtyard—and how it had seemed to her, if only for a moment, that they were defacing the carvings rather than repairing them.

Was there a connection or was she jumping to conclusions? And even if she was right, did her observation have any significance with regard to their mission?

"Sir," she said finally, "I may be completely off base, but I think the Rithrim are making some changes in their public statuary policy."

He looked at her. "What do you mean?"

"Back in the courtyard, there were some builders—"

"I remember," he said. "I saw them working on one of the reliefs."

"That's right," Uhura confirmed. "At first I thought they were just doing some repairs. Then it occurred to me that they might be obliterating what was there. And now, seeing these statues missing, I'm wondering if there isn't some sweeping change taking place in Rithramen society—some philosophical overhaul that requires them to reject figures they used to honor."

The commodore's brow furrowed. "Makes sense. And if that's the case, I'd like to know about it. It may be nothing of concern to us, of course. But then again, it may be significant—if not now, then down the line."

Uhura agreed. "Maybe we should ask the governors," she suggested.

Wesley nodded. "Maybe we should." Taking out his communicator, he flipped it open. "Two to beam up," he instructed the transporter chief.

But before the order went into effect, Uhura noticed, he took a last glance at the gaps in the statuary. Nor could she help but look that way herself.

"Damnedest thing," said the commodore just before they left the procreation center behind.

Back in her quarters, Uhura stood in front of the bathroom mirror and ran a comb through her hair, grateful for the opportunity that Wesley had afforded her to shower and change her clothes. It felt good to be clean again, to be wearing a freshly laundered uniform and to hear nothing but the subtle hum of the *Lexington*'s engines, after the relentless furor of Girin Gatha.

Fortunately the commodore hadn't deemed the missing-statuary question so urgent that they had to contact the governors immediately. The lieutenant grimaced now at the idea of having to wear her perspiration-soiled one-piece through an extended session with Endris and the others.

Considering herself one last time in the mirror, she put down her brush, smoothed her uniform, and left the bathroom. The lights, she knew, would switch off a few moments after the room's sensors recorded her absence.

Wesley had asked her to be on the bridge in half an hour; she had ten minutes left. But with nothing to keep her here, and the answers to her questions awaiting, Uhura decided to report early.

She was halfway to the door when she heard the beeping that signaled the presence of someone outside. It surprised her. Who could it be? she wondered.

"Come on in," said the communications officer.

As the doors slid aside, they revealed Jerome Baila. His expression was as guarded as ever, Uhura noted. But there was something different about his eyes— something soft, almost vulnerable, where before they'd been hard and unyielding.

Taking a step inside, he said: "Can I talk to you?"

She shrugged. "Sure. I'm due on the bridge soon, but I can spare a few minutes. Have a seat, won't you?"

Baila crossed to the overstuffed chair in one corner of the room and sat down on the forward edge of it. Uhura positioned herself just opposite, on the chair's twin. There was a free-form glass table between them, supported by more of that real wood that had so impressed her when she arrived here.

"What can I do for you?" she asked.

His one hand kneaded the other; the man seemed full to brimming with nervous energy. "Tell me about your village," he said. "Your family. What kind of place you come from."

After he'd kept her at such a distance until now, these weren't exactly the kinds of questions Uhura had expected. She was tempted to ask about the change of tack—but refrained.

"I come from Koyo," she told him. "It's a small town just west of Mombasa, though not so far west the ground's not good for farming. My father is a professor of African history with the University of Kenya; my mother was a sculptress. I was their only child." She paused. "What else would you like to know?"

"Where did you learn sign language?" he asked.

Uhura smiled as she thought about it. "When I was ten, my cousin Epala came to stay with us for a summer. Epala had been deaf since birth; she spoke with her hands. I remember thinking they were like flitting birds, and that I would never understand what she was saying. But she was older than I was by a year, and very pretty, and I wanted to be just like her. So I learned the language of the flitting birds." Her smile grew broader. "In fact, that's what first got me interested in communications."

Baila nodded. "And what did they think, this family of yours, when you decided to go out into space?"

She shrugged. "They weren't thrilled about it at first; it meant I'd be gone for long periods at a time. But they accepted it after a while." She looked at him. "Why?"

He swallowed. "I just wanted to know." And much to her surprise, he got up and headed for the door.

"Whoa—hang on just a moment there!" The words were out of her mouth before she knew it. And they weren't the kind she usually spoke. There was a distinct tinge of anger to them.

Baila stopped, turned. "Yes?" His eyes were opaque again, arrogant. His very bearing was a challenge.

For a moment, as Uhura's anger subsided, she wondered what she was going to say next. Why was she angry, anyway? What had he done but ask her some questions?

No, he'd done more than that. He'd asked her for a part of herself. And in that request had been an implicit assurance that he would give something of himself in exchange. Now he was trying to renege on that promise, but she wasn't going to let him get away with it.

"You asked," she told him, "and I answered. Now it's my turn. *Sit.*"

Baila hesitated, but only for an instant. Then he did as he was told.

Uhura sat down again, too. She looked her visitor square in the eye and asked: "Where are *you* from?"

The muscles in his temples worked ever so slightly. "Potayu. Near Lake Nyasa."

"And your background?" She could see that she was going to have to drag it out of him.

"My father was a farmer, my mother a farmer as well. I have six brothers and sisters. And the ground there was never as good for farming as it was near Mombasa."

He spoke the last words like a whip, as if it were her fault his family hadn't had an easy time of it. Uhura, like any East African, was familiar with the crop failures that had taken place a decade ago around Nyasa. She couldn't help it if she'd lived in a more fertile area.

"You make it sound as if I was the one who withheld the rain," she said.

He shrugged. "That wasn't my intention."

Uhura bristled at his insolence, but she still wanted to understand him. In fact, she wanted to pierce that attitude of his more than ever now.

What else might she ask him? Then she remembered the last thing *he'd* asked *her.* "What did your family think of your joining Starfleet?"

Before she'd gotten the last word out, Uhura saw the look in his eyes. It was relief, she realized. He'd *wanted* her to pose that question, hadn't he? That was what he'd been angling for all along.

"They disapproved," he told her. "They disapproved mightily."

Bits and pieces of information Uhura had heard as a child floated to the surface of her memory. And suddenly she understood. She understood everything.

"Potayu was one of the towns that followed Beccah Talulu, wasn't it?"

"It was," he admitted. "My parents were among her first and most loyal supporters. They took up her ways even before I was born."

"So when the crops failed—"

"We starved," he said, finishing the thought for her. "No one actually died, of course, but a lot of us came close. And if the rains hadn't finally come when they did . . . I probably wouldn't be here talking to you now."

Uhura shook her head. It was the twenty-third century. People weren't supposed to starve to death, or even come close. But Beccah Talulu had persuaded entire villages to give up the techniques of modern science and embrace the primitive virtues she espoused.

Not that it had been *all* bad. Civilization had a way of distancing people from their roots; it was a good thing to be reminded of one's kinship with nature. But Talulu, a self-styled prophetess who claimed to be descended from the great kings of the region, went too far, it seemed to Uhura.

"As a child," Baila said, "I wasn't allowed to read about anything even vaguely scientific. But I had this curiosity—this desire to know about things beyond our town and its ways. So when my parents took me into one of the larger towns to sell their baskets and their pottery in the market, I stole from the booksellers and hid the books in my robes. After a while I got quite good at it. But the books didn't satisfy—they only fanned my desire."

His eyes flickered, as if he were reliving everything he was saying. "Finally, when I was eleven, I couldn't contain myself anymore. I ran away to my aunt's house in Quelimane. My aunt didn't approve of Talulu. She was more than glad to have me."

Uhura looked at him. "Quelimane is on the coast. You traveled all the way there from Potayu—at the age of eleven?"

He grunted. "It was the longest journey I ever made. Earth to the Klingon Neutral Zone seems like a short hop by comparison. But I made it."

"What about your parents?" she asked. "Didn't they want you back?"

Baila shook his head. "Aunt Kisal told them why I left. They didn't try to convince me I was wrong. They just wrote me off."

Such a thing was incomprehensible to Uhura. She couldn't imagine parents who would give up their child without a fight. But then, she hadn't lived in a Talulu village, had she?

"Thanks to my aunt," he went on, "I had a proper education. And I fell in love with the idea of Starfleet —of going out where no one had gone before. Sometimes I couldn't sleep for thinking about it. I worked hard. I worked *very* hard. And on my second try, I made it into the Academy."

"Your aunt must have been very proud," Uhura commented.

He shook his head. "My aunt passed away before I

was accepted." He sighed. "My first year at the Academy was fascinating, exciting, but very lonely. No matter how many friends I made, there was a void in my spirit that cried out for the woman who'd raised me." He licked his lips. "When summer break came, all the other cadets went home to their families. I had no one to go home to, but I desperately didn't want to stay in San Francisco all by myself. And then I had an idea: I would go back to Potayu."

"You went?" she asked.

Baila nodded. "I went. But as it turned out, it wasn't a very good idea. My parents, my brothers and sisters . . . they acted as if they didn't know me. It was as if I'd never existed for them. And when I protested that I was still *me,* I was still Jerome, my mother said that Jerome was long dead and that the dead don't come back to life, no matter what I'd been taught in the great Academy.

"You see," he said, "it was so long since I'd been there, I'd forgotten what Beccah Talulu had said about going out to the stars in ships: that it was wrong, that it was an insult to the soil that gave us birth. My family believed that what I was doing, what I was planning to do, was an act against nature." He hung his head, and the muscles in his temples worked even harder than before; when he spoke, it was ever so softly. "After all, Beccah Talulu had said so."

Uhura regarded him. There was no haughtiness left in him, no arrogance. There was only a man who had been cut off from his past and his people—a man who, in gaining what he believed was his heart's desire, had lost all that was dear to him.

He looked up, his chiseled nostrils flaring. "So now

you know," he told her. "You've heard a story I didn't dare tell to anyone on this ship. And make no mistake, if you hadn't come from Koyo near Mombasa, I wouldn't have told you, either."

She understood. There was no need to say so.

What was it Commodore Wesley had asked her, back at the procreation center? "Can you tell me what's made him stop caring?" he had said. "He used to be a good officer—a very good officer. And now he's something less than that."

Uhura knew the answer to the commodore's question now. Slowly but surely, Baila's dedication had been undermined by his heartsickness. His curiosity had been ground down by his family's disapproval of what he'd become. And over the long years the loss had made a husk out of him, a hollowed-out imitation of an officer.

Baila stood. "We're probably overdue on the bridge," he told her. "We should be getting up there."

She cursed inwardly. She'd been so enthralled by Baila's confession, she'd forgotten all about Wesley's orders. Shooting to her feet, she headed for the door. But before she got halfway, she noticed her companion hadn't moved.

"Something wrong?" she asked.

He held her with his gaze. "What I told you—it goes no farther than this room. I don't want anyone else to know."

Uhura frowned. It was a confidence; she hadn't planned to discuss it with anyone anyway. "No one else," she agreed.

He nodded. "Thank you."

Then they went out the door and headed for the turbolift.

The *Enterprise* dropped out of warp space, and the first thing Kirk saw were large pieces of metal floating in front of them. The debris appeared to be the remains of some sort of ship, and for a fleeting moment Kirk thought that some starship had arrived ahead of them, perhaps even dispatched the raiders before they could engage in their terrorist activities.

"Spock—"

"Analyzing debris, Captain," Spock reported, anticipating Kirk's request. It took only a few moments before he looked up from the science station. "It would appear to be the remains of the *Viking*, Captain."

Kirk cursed to himself. The *Viking*, the patrol ship that had come to offer aid to Gamma Xaridian IV, although it turned out there was none to be given. What had been the captain's plan, then? Had the *Viking* and its crew remained in the system, perhaps hidden themselves nearby, waiting to see if the raiders would strike again? Whatever had been their intention, that act of bravery had been their last.

Kirk's blood boiled as he said, "Ahead full."

"Approaching Gamma Xaridian Eight, Captain," Sulu called out.

And suddenly Chekov was pointing at the screen, almost jumping to his feet. "There they are!"

"Imprecise but enthusiastic, Mr. Chekov," said Kirk. "There they are indeed."

The raiders were swarming toward the eighth planet

of the Gamma Xaridian system, and the sensors quickly determined that their number was an even dozen.

"They appear to be arriving only now," said Spock. "It would seem that the *Viking*'s battle tactics were able to slow the raiders down sufficiently so that the emergency signal reached us in time."

"Let's make sure that *Viking*'s sacrifice wasn't in vain," said Kirk sharply. "Uhu—Palmer, open a channel. Warn them off from Gamma Xaridian Eight."

"Hailing them on all frequencies, Captain," said Palmer. "No reply."

And suddenly the raiding ships came together, angled around, and hurtled directly toward the *Enterprise*.

"I think we're about to get their reply," said Kirk.

The raiders dived toward them in two staggered rows of six, and then their weapons came alive, raking the much larger starship with a series of hammerlike blasts that shook the *Enterprise* over and over.

"Repeated hits on the starboard shield!" Sulu called out.

"All phasers, fire!" called Kirk.

The *Enterprise* phasers lashed out at the foremost of the ships—but a split second before there was contact, the raiders peeled away from one another, gracefully forming twin arcs, and the phaser blasts went straight up the middle, passing them by harmlessly.

"Stay ahead of them, Mr. Sulu," said Kirk. "Anticipate their moves and fire where they're going to be."

Chekov looked at Sulu nervously and whispered, "He wants you to read their minds?"

Sulu made no reply. Instead his fingers flew over the targeting devices as he watched carefully the sweeping curves of one set of the ships. Mentally he counted down, looked to where their course was going to take them, and fired.

And the half dozen ships, incredibly, suddenly angled down and away, dodging the phaser blast with only kilometers to spare.

Meanwhile the other half dozen ships swept in from port and again fired on the *Enterprise,* blasting away and then shooting off into the either before the starship could return fire.

"Starboard and port shields each down seventy percent," reported Spock.

Kirk grimaced upon hearing the news. Draining off power from one shield to supplement the other would leave them virtually unprotected on one side. "Status on the raiders?"

"We have yet to hit any of them. The size of their engines would not indicate warp capabilities above factor two, but they are far more maneuverable at impulse than we are. Their size and speed make it possible for them to stay extremely close to the ship and increase the effectiveness of their weapons without suffering damage from ours. Their fighting style does not correlate with any known tactics."

"They're coming up behind us!"

"Bring us around!"

"Too late!"

The raiders hammered them from aft. Kirk could almost hear the screams from the engineering section; the shield generators were stretched to the breaking point.

"Phaser and photon array, full spread! Fire!"

The *Enterprise* cut loose with all the armament at its command, and with speed and maneuvering that bordered on the supernatural, the raiders danced in between the bursts from the mighty starship. In the meantime the ship shook yet again; its defenses were wearing down quickly.

Damage reports were being screamed to the bridge from all parts of the ship. "Forward phasers out!" called Spock. "Starboard shields buckling. Port shields can sustain only another hit or two."

"Keptin, the Turnoga defense!" Chekov suddenly shouted. "In a situation like this—"

"Not now, Mr. Chekov!" said Kirk.

"But, sir, against multiple enemies, the Turnoga defense—"

"That's for use against vessels considerably larger than these, Ensign, and I don't have time to turn the bridge into an Academy lecture hall. Bring us around at four-nineteen mark six. Drop forward shields, prepare for warp speed."

"What?" Chekov couldn't believe it. "Captain, even minimal warp will kick us right out of the system! The colony will be defenseless. And with no shields, *we'll* be defenseless. They could fire on us before—"

"Carry out your orders, Ensign!"

"Yes, sir!" But even as his hands flew over the controls, he continued. "But I know if we adapted Turnoga—"

"Ensign, you're relieved," said Kirk sharply. "Palmer, take over. Mr. Chekov, get the hell off the bridge. You're confined to quarters."

Chekov's hands froze, and he felt the blood pounding through his head. He tried to get words out, and then Palmer was at his side, shoving on his shoulder. The Russian staggered to his feet, the world seeming to swirl around him, and from a distance he heard Palmer saying, "Course laid in, sir."

"Bring us ahead, full impulse."

As Chekov moved to the turbolift, he saw Dr. McCoy standing there. The ensign had been so focused on the battle, he hadn't even noticed the CMO arrive on the bridge. Saying nothing, Chekov shoved past him into the lift.

But he wasn't getting rid of McCoy so easily. "Come on," said the doctor. "I'll escort you to your quarters." And without waiting for a response, McCoy followed him into the lift.

Putting the incident with Chekov aside, Kirk focused on the task at hand. The raiding ships had come together again, and the *Enterprise* was on a collision course with the small fleet.

"They aren't firing," Palmer said in surprise.

"It's because we dropped our shields. They don't know whether we're surrendering or just suicidal. On my order I'll want warp four."

"Direct acceleration, Captain?" Sulu half turned in his chair. "Sir, the stress could—" But Kirk's expression prompted Sulu simply to turn back to his station and say, "Aye, sir."

They drew closer and closer to the raiders, until the smaller, hovering ships were filling the screen.

Kirk punched his direct line to the engine room. "Scotty!"

"Aye, Captain!" The chief engineer sounded even

more beleaguered than usual. Not surprising, considering the circumstances.

"On my order I want you to reroute all power from the rear deflectors and shore up the forward."

"We'll have our tails hanging out, sir."

"I know that, Mr. Scott. Get ready."

Still the raiders seemed to hesitate, uncertain of what sort of trick the *Enterprise* might have up its sleeve.

"Collision course," said Sulu. "Counting down, eleven . . . ten . . . nine . . . eight . . . seven . . . six . . . Raiders are bringing their weapons on line."

"Now, Scotty! Reroute shields!"

The deflectors to the rear of the *Enterprise* faded almost to nonexistence, and the forward shields powered up. Several experimental blasts from the raiders bounced harmlessly off the starship's forward defenses.

Realizing that the *Enterprise* was now in a position to ram right through them, the raiders performed the same maneuver they had used earlier—they split off, coming in tight on both sides of the starship.

"Sir, they're coming in right on top of us!"

Kirk counted under his breath and then shouted, "Now, Sulu! Full ahead, warp four!"

The *Enterprise* leaped forward. The crew slammed back in their seats, and all around Kirk were the sounds of the ship's infrastructure creaking under the sudden acceleration.

"Captain!" Spock shouted over the roar of the engines. "Seven of the raiders were caught in our warp field when we accelerated!"

"Excellent!" Kirk bellowed back. "Sulu, slow us down! Take us out of warp!"

Obediently the mighty engines of the *Enterprise* reversed, and warp space began to break up around the ship. And so, too, did the ships of the raiders. Pieces flew apart everywhere as the ships shuddered, trembled, and burst apart.

"They couldn't stand the stress of warp four!" said Palmer in amazement.

"I surmised as much, since their engines weren't designed to exceed warp two," said Kirk briskly. "Because they were staying so close to our hull, I thought we could drag them along if we hit fast into warp space. Palmer, plot a course back to Gamma Xaridian Four."

"Already got it, Captain."

"Good. Mr. Sulu, best possible speed. Get us there in one piece but quickly. Some of them managed to slip past us, and we'll still have them to deal with."

The *Enterprise* swung around and an instant later was hurtling back through space. They arrived on the outskirts of the Gamma Xaridian system just as the remaining raiders were pulling themselves back together.

The sight of the returning starship clearly unnerved the smaller ships; they started to peel off in all directions, and all of those directions were away from Gamma Xaridian VIII. Obviously they had had enough for one day.

Kirk, however, was not quite finished. "Tractor beams, widest possible field!" he called. Spreading the tractors that wide would weaken their overall effect, but the ships were small enough that it might not take that much to hold them.

And as it turned out, it didn't. One of the ships was just a hair too slow, and before it could put enough distance between itself and the *Enterprise,* it had been snagged by the tractor beams.

"Got it, Captain!" Sulu crowed.

"Reel them in, Mr. Sulu. Let's see if any of their friends come to rescue them."

Such was not to be the case. The other ships hurtled away, leaving the one captive and at the mercy of the starship. At the moment Kirk wasn't feeling particularly merciful. Nevertheless, he saw his opportunity: he could now find out who was behind these destructive and seemingly random raids on the Xaridian colonies.

"Open a hailing frequency to—"

And at that moment the trapped raider ship blew up. It was all the *Enterprise*'s weakened shields could do to protect the starship from the surprisingly large blast that the ship generated. As it was, the overburdened forward shields went down completely. So all-consuming was the destruction that there weren't even fragments of the raider ship left. Within moments space around them was empty. The other raiders had disappeared in a variety of directions, and the one that they had captured had exploded in their face.

Chapter Eight

McCoy STOLE A GLANCE at Chekov. The ensign had remained silent for the entirety of the turbolift ride. Then again, what could he say? He'd made a mistake, and a big one.

When they reached deck six, where Chekov's quarters were situated, the ensign turned to him. "You don't have to keep me company anymore. I am all right, I assure you."

The doctor shook his head. "Nothing doing. I said I'd escort you to your quarters, and that's what I intend to do."

Sighing, the Russian headed for his cabin. The corridors were very, very quiet, McCoy noted. The deck was mostly crew quarters, double rooms for all, but during a red alert, few of the crew were in their rooms.

It occurred to the doctor that he rarely visited this deck, since most patients came to his sickbay. Still, the silence was uncanny. That would certainly be tough on Chekov, he mused.

Before long they'd reached the ensign's cabin. The doors slid aside for them, and they entered.

Once inside, Chekov took a seat by the desk while McCoy leaned against a dresser, his arms folded across his chest. The doctor looked around. He'd forgotten how cramped it could be in a younger officer's quarters.

Ah, well, he thought, at least it was better than the hammock and kit bag sailors started off with centuries ago. He paused, reconsidering the place. Not by much, though.

"Well, Chekov, what now?"

"Do we maintain a firing squad?" the younger man asked.

"Of course not. Why?"

"Because the keptin vill vant to assemble one after ve get out of this."

"Poppycock. You screwed up. Big deal. We all do it sooner or later; you just did it at a worse time than others. Something about you navigators, always going off half-cocked and getting yourselves into trouble. First Bailey, then Styles, then Riley, and now you. Is it something they teach at the Academy?"

"No, Doctor. I . . . I just can't explain it. I vas sure I had the right maneuver and—"

"And you picked the wrong time to tell Captain Kirk. Maybe you've been through too few red alerts to understand. Simulations are close, but never confuse them with the real thing. There are times and places for making suggestions to the captain—and when we're surrounded by marauders isn't one of them."

"I knew that," Chekov began helplessly. He looked as if he was going to try again, but instead he slumped into a brooding silence. Staring at the table top, the ensign ignored the doctor.

McCoy moved around the room for a moment, trying to find the right tack to take. Chekov was feeling bad enough, and he did not want to push him too far one way or another. Still, the psychiatrist in him didn't want to leave until he could ease Chekov's pain, even a little.

"Chekov, the captain had his own options to consider." He stopped himself when he saw the ensign's reaction. Though what he'd said was true, it wasn't the right approach. And then another one occurred to him. "How did you do on the *Kobayashi Maru* test?"

There was a long pause. "I blew up my ship," Chekov said finally. He hung his head. "At the time I thought I was being original. Took the Klingons with me, too."

"You sacrificed yourself and your ship?" McCoy asked incredulously.

Chekov let out a long sigh and nodded.

"That certainly was unique." McCoy walked over and leaned forward, making sure he was in Chekov's peripheral vision. "Son, you'll learn. And you'll learn quickly. You never would have made it to deep space if Command didn't think you were ready. There must be a demon or two you need to knock out of your head. And then it'll be clear sailing."

The doctor then sat down right beside Chekov and leaned over. He lowered his voice to an almost conspiratorial whisper.

"I'll let you in on a little secret. Do you remember that Captain Kirk had to take the same test you did? Face the no-win scenario?"

"Of course," came the soft reply.

"Do you know how the captain did?"

"I guess he lasted a long time and then lost. Everyone does."

"Oh, no, Ensign," McCoy said. And for a moment Chekov's head bobbed up. The doctor flashed him a happy grin and said, "Oh sure, he did that the first two times. But he insisted on a third trial—and you know what he did *then?*"

Chekov only shook his head.

"He sneaked in and, with some help, reprogrammed the computers. He actually beat the scenario."

"Vhat?" Chekov stared at McCoy as if the doctor had suddenly sprouted a third arm.

"I'm told no one ever did that before. And they certainly saw to it that no one would do it again. Now, can you keep that to yourself?"

"Yes, sir." McCoy could see Chekov pondering the fact: Kirk had beaten the game by rewriting the rules. Such thinking had probably never occurred to him.

"Now, you get some rest. If you need me, come on down. Door's always open." Satisfied he'd done some good, the doctor knocked on the desk top twice with his knuckles and walked out of the cabin.

* * *

Chekov looked up after the door slid closed with its familiar whoosh, and shook his head. Kirk had beaten the Kobayashi Maru!

The ensign tried to rerun the standard command test in his mind. There was the disabled ship in Klingon territory. When his turn had come, he chose to send his ship, the *Yorktown* into the Neutral Zone to perform a rescue mission. Then all of a sudden he was surrounded. He remembered gripping the command chair arms with his hands. The sweat began to bead on his brow from phantom memory. . . .

Engineering reported casualties and coolant leaks. His medical officer reported radiation burns and casualties already in double digits. The *Yorktown* managed to weaken the shields on one Klingon ship before his own shields were down to critical limits.

His voice, calling the self-destruct sequence, echoed in his mind. He had to shout down his first officer, Ravi Akbar, who adamantly refused to give the code authorization. Then the countdown and the blinding white lights. . . .

It was a month before Akbar was civil to him again.

Chekov strained to imagine which part of the computer program Kirk rewrote to allow him to win. Was it the number of enemy vessels? The strength of his own ship? How did Kirk come up with such thoughts at the tender age of twenty? With much to ponder, he returned to his bunk, thankful that his roommate was at Weapons Control and wouldn't be back for a while.

A long while, thanks to the blunder of a young navigator named Pavel Chekov.

* * *

As Uhura emerged from the turbolift with Baila a step behind her, Wesley glanced in their direction. While casual on the surface, his scrutiny conveyed the intended meaning. Officers were not to report late to his bridge—unless they had a damned good excuse.

However, as she didn't *have* a good excuse, Uhura simply made her way to the commodore's side and stood there silent. She could hear the soft padding of Baila's boots behind her as he exchanged places with the communications officer from the previous shift.

Wesley seemed intent on the viewscreen, with its sweep of Rithramen landscape. But he wasn't nearly as intent as he seemed.

"You're a little tardy," he acknowledged, rubbing it in—though he spoke too softly for anyone but Uhura to hear him.

"It won't happen again," she assured him, also sotto voce.

He looked up at her, the beginnings of a smile softening the line of his mouth. "Good. Then we can get to the bottom of this statuary question." Without turning, he addressed his communications officer, who'd barely had a moment to settle in. "Raise present-cycle governor Endris, Mr. Baila."

"Aye, sir," came the response.

It took a while for Endris to appear. Which was understandable, Uhura mused, given the fact that the Rithrim weren't expecting a communication right now. As she waited, she went over the kinds of signals she might use to convey their curiosity about the statues.

Abruptly the image on the viewscreen shifted, and

there was Endris. As before, he was surrounded by the kind of brightness that made Uhura squint.

"Greetings," said the Rithrim. "I have been told you wish to speak with me." His hands posed the question: why?

Wesley smiled. "Nothing terribly important, I think. However, part of the reason we're here is to gain a better understanding of your people, and if we're to understand you, we must ask questions."

There was no need for Uhura to do very much; the words would speak for themselves, even to a Rithrim.

"I agree," Endris assured him. His gestures underlined the sentiment.

"Good," said the commodore. He cleared his throat. "Back at the procreation center, I couldn't help but notice the statuary around the building. Fine workmanship, too. But it looked as if some statues had been removed." He leaned forward slightly in his seat. "Is there a reason for that?"

This time Uhura had a bigger part to play. She had to expand on Wesley's praise for the statues, then make his request as polite as possible.

Whether it was her doing or not, the Rithrim seemed unperturbed by the query. "The conditions at Girin Gatha have not been kind to some of the statuary," he explained. "We have found it necessary to repair or replace certain pieces." His signs invited further inquiries if Wesley thought they would be productive; Uhura said as much.

The commodore shook his head. "No. I think we've got our answer. Thank you for your patience, Present-cycle Governor." The lieutenant embellished the expression of gratitude.

"It was no trouble," Endris told him. His expression seemed to change subtly; likewise, Uhura noted, the position of his hands. "Unfortunately, I must convey some news you may not find pleasing."

A crease developed in the center of Wesley's forehead. "Oh?"

The Rithrim clearly didn't know how to respond to that. Uhura used her signs to turn it into an appeal for additional information.

"There has been an alteration of plans," said the governor. "We have decided against providing a site for your observation facility." He eloquently indicated his regrets. "I hope this does not represent a great inconvenience."

Uhura didn't get it. Apparently neither did the commodore; the crease in his brow grew more distinct.

"I'm at a loss," said Wesley. "If I may ask, what happened to change your minds?"

Even before Endris spoke, Uhura could tell by his sign language that he was loath to disclose any more. "I am not at liberty to discuss the matter further," the Rithrim told them. "Again, I apologize for the inconvenience."

The commodore took a breath, let it out. "Have we offended you in some way?"

"In *no* way have you offended us."

Stymied, Wesley looked up at Uhura. "Any idea what's going on here?" he asked, keeping his voice to a whisper.

She shook her head. "I wish I did, sir."

Wesley turned back to the screen. "How does this decision affect what we're doing at Girin Gatha?"

Uhura added a question: Will we be allowed to continue our work there?

Endris appeared to hesitate. Finally he said: "We will no longer require your assistance at the procreation center. I believed I had made that clear; if not, allow me to make it clear now."

The commodore held his hands out, as if in a plea for sanity. "Present-cycle Governor, we're willing to help you with your problem *regardless* of what happens to our observatory. If you recall, I said those were separate issues."

Uhura did her best to emphasize the concept of separateness. It seemed to have no effect.

"I can only repeat our position on this point," the Rithrim replied. His gestures made it clear there was no room for debate—a fact which she conveyed to Wesley.

Nonetheless, the commodore wasn't one to take no for an answer. Fixing Endris with his gaze, he chose his words carefully. "While I concede that this is your world and that it's your right to do what you want with it, I would be remiss if I didn't remind you that there are lives at stake here—those of your *young,* no less. If I were in your position, I would be reluctant indeed to make any decision that jeopardized those lives." He paused. "It's been my experience that any difference can be worked out, any obstacle to cooperation overcome, if both parties are committed to the task. I cannot imagine that this instance would prove an exception."

The Rithrim's signs were firm—unyielding almost to the point of rudeness. "You may remain in orbit around our world while you recover your people and

131

your equipment," he said. "Then you must leave, albeit with our thanks for your kindness."

"I don't believe this," Wesley muttered. "They're going to send us away—let innocents *die* when we could help them—without even telling us why. It's absurd."

Uhura felt the same way. But neither she nor the commodore could do anything about it, because in the next moment Endris's visage vanished, to be replaced by the majestic image of Rithra.

The raiders streaked through space and started firing on the *Enterprise,* their weapons exploding off the ship's hull.

"Freeze it."

Obediently the raiders' ships came to a halt.

In the conference room, Kirk, Spock, McCoy, Scotty, Sulu, and Giotto sat around the table, staring at the frozen image on the central computer screen.

"Would have been a bonny thing if we could have done that during the battle," said Scotty ruefully.

There was glum nodding of heads.

"Analysis, gentlemen," said Kirk. "What are we dealing with here?"

"We've run a thorough analysis on the types of weapon discharges used during the battle," said Spock. "Without any question, these are the same individuals who struck at the colony at Alpha Xaridian Two and, presumably, the other colonies as well. The radiation traces are unmistakable."

"But we still don't have any record of who uses weaponry of that sort."

Spock shook his head. "Nothing directly. Furthermore the ship design"—he indicated the odd angles of the ship—"is unique in Federation records. Either this is a race that we have never before encountered or else they have customized their ships in order to disguise their origins."

"And did they customize their sensor and helm abilities as well?" Sulu wondered out loud. "I've never seen maneuvering like that."

"How fast were they going?" asked Kirk. "It almost seemed as if they were going faster than impulse power but below sublight—at some sort of bizarre speed in between."

But Scotty was shaking his head. "No. That's not it at all. One of the lads ran a graphics breakdown. Computer: File Pavel-One, please."

The computer screen immediately switched to an image of one of the raiders, with a blue grid superimposed on it. The ship was positioned in the right-hand corner of the screen.

"Run the graphics, please," said Scotty.

The ship, a frame at a time, made its way from the upper right to the center of the screen and then veered off to the lower left. Another raider following precisely the same trajectory was visible coming in behind it. A trailing red line that delineated the ship's course was left behind, and at nine points along the line there were small boxes with numbers next to them.

"Now you'll see here"—Scotty indicated the upper right—"that when we first start tracking the ship, it's moving at zero-point-eight light speed. A nice clip, I'll be granting ye that . . . but not warp speed. And the speed remains steady along all these points, until here"—and he tapped the center of the screen—"where she suddenly changes course like a bat out of hell."

"How fast was it going then?" asked Kirk. He leaned forward and blinked in surprise. "Zero-point-eight? It didn't change speed?"

"No, sir. Not at any time during its arc."

Giotto whistled. Sulu and McCoy leaned forward, staring in disbelief. "Can you run that thing at normal speed?" asked McCoy.

"Computer," said Scotty, "run graphic at normal speed."

McCoy blinked and almost missed it. "Incredible."

"The way they were going, I took it for granted that they were changing speeds," said Sulu. "I was amazed at the technology they had that enabled them to accelerate and brake so quickly."

"Well, they dinna have it," said Scotty. "Incredible skill and precision in maneuvering, yes, like nothing I've ever seen. But their speed is constant."

Kirk nodded. Well, at least we're beginning to have some idea of what we're up against. Mr. Scott, my compliments to whichever one of your lads worked up that computer study. That was good thinking."

"Yes, well,"—Scotty cleared his throat loudly—"he isn't exactly one of *my* lads. He's one of yours, actually. And he had some time on his hands, what with his being confined to quarters."

For a moment Kirk frowned, having no idea what Scotty was talking about. Then the light dawned. "Chekov."

"Aye."

"Yes, well . . ." Kirk harrumphed slightly and then said, "Good work on his part. I knew he was in Starfleet for *some* reason."

Sulu spoke up. "I'll let him know you were pleased, Captain."

"Yes, Mr. Sulu. You do that."

Chapter Nine

SITTING AT HIS DESK, Chekov engaged the ship's computer in yet another battle simulation. On the screen a red blip representing the *Enterprise* maneuvered against a series of yellow blips, which stood for the marauders.

Thinking about the *Kobayashi Maru* test and how Kirk reprogrammed the simulation had set the ensign to thinking. At the Academy he had studied the use of computer models; it had just never occurred to him before to actually use them on the *Enterprise*.

What was more, he was finding it infinitely instructive. The first time he ran the program, Chekov followed Kirk's actions and watched a near-perfect repeat of what actually happened.

Then he asked the computer to implement his own maneuver and watched for the results. They were the same each and every time: a victory for the *Enterprise,* hands down.

Chekov had been right. And his idol, Captain Kirk, had been wrong—though it was unlikely the ensign would ever get any satisfaction from the knowledge.

He was about to store the last simulation when the door buzzer sounded. Given his level of concentration, it startled him, but only for a moment.

"Come in," he said, steeling himself.

After all, he expected to see Kirk or Spock, ready to rake him over the coals for his actions up on the bridge. He was surprised and relieved to see the smiling face of Sulu instead.

"Hi there, Ensign. We missed you at the briefing, and I thought you should know what's going on."

"You mean they haven't kicked me off the bridge yet?"

Sulu's smile broadened as he sat down on the edge of Chekov's bed. "No. But I can imagine the captain is pretty sore about what happened. You know, Pavel, he had every right to discipline you after that stunt you pulled."

"But my plan would have worked. Here—look."

Chekov leaned back in his chair and had the computer rerun the last computer simulation. As Sulu watched, the red blip representing the *Enterprise* emerged victorious.

"See?" asked the ensign, when it was all over.

The navigator shook his head. "You don't get it, do you? You weren't in command, Pavel—the *captain* was. It was red alert. Attacking ships were flying around like butterflies, and you stopped everything to offer a suggestion."

"Did you really think Captain Kirk would call a time-out to discuss the merits of your plan—even if it *was* sounder than his?" The navigator paused to let his words sink in. "As long as the captain's in command, he's got to call the shots. You know full well that when there's time, he'll ask the bridge for suggestions and opinions. But they must be offered when the time is right. Understand?"

Chekov thought about it. At last he nodded. "Yes. I think I do. Thank you. But where do we go from here?"

"At the briefing the captain decided that we're going to find those ships again—but this time we'll be better prepared to deal with them. We all know they must be stopped before they destroy another colony.

"In the meantime we're on yellow alert and Spock is riding the sensor teams real hard, making sure we scan for every possible emission trace. We'll find those raiders—it's just a matter of when."

"Do I still have a job up there?" Chekov asked, nodding upward.

"I think you'll be riding the board again before you know it." Sulu smiled once again, and Chekov was impressed at how such a simple gesture could transform his mood. He found himself feeling a bit better.

"I hope so. Othervise I may as vell start filing for a transfer." He frowned. "If I've lost Keptin Kirk's confidence, then there's no place for me here."

Sulu stood and said, "True. But don't forget: he's left you on the duty roster, and he still hasn't been down to take you to task. Those are both good signs. Now I'm going to catch some sleep, just in case. See you back upstairs." With that, he patted Chekov on the back and left the cabin.

Chekov glanced at his chronometer and realized his shift was due to begin in a short while. He quickly shut off the simulation scenario and called up the active-duty roster. To his relief he was still scheduled for a shift on the bridge. A quick change of uniform, some water to help smooth down his longish hair, and Pavel Chekov was ready to report for duty.

Uhura sat on a stool in sickbay and watched Dr. Coss shake his head. "I don't get it, Commodore. We're supposed to pack up and take off, just like that?"

Wesley nodded. "I'm afraid so." Absently he picked up a medical tricorder and examined it. "That's what the present-cycle governor has asked us to do, and we have no choice but to comply."

Coss sputtered. "That's insane. Those people have got a serious problem on their hands—one that's likely to produce a whole slew of birth defects, not to mention claim some lives—and they're turning down help it'd cost them nothing to accept?"

"That's about the size of it," said the commodore.

The doctor turned to Uhura. "Are we missing something here, Lieutenant? Could we be misinterpreting their message somehow?"

She shook her head. "It's pretty clear. They just don't want us on their planet."

"But they wanted us a few hours ago. What's different now? What's changed?"

Wesley shrugged. "Damned if *I* know. It's a mystery, Doctor. And as much as I hate leaving a mystery unsolved, we've got to—"

"Commodore?" It was Baila's voice coming over the intercom.

"Yes, Lieutenant?"

"Sir, I'm receiving a call from the Rithrim."

Wesley grunted. "From Endris?"

"Maybe they've come to their senses," muttered Coss.

"No, sir," came Baila's response. "Not from Endris. In fact, it's not from the governors at all. It's from a *procreator.*"

The commodore exchanged glances with Uhura. "Come on, Lieutenant. You're with me."

"And so am I," the doctor insisted. "I want to know what's going on here."

As they left sickbay and headed for the bridge, Uhura could feel her pulse accelerate. For a procreator to want to speak with them directly, something *big* had to be in the offing.

When Chekov walked back onto the bridge, he felt as if all eyes were on him. Fortunately Scotty had the conn; Kirk and Spock were off somewhere else; likewise Sulu and Palmer. Thanking the Fates for small favors, the ensign briskly crossed the bridge and took his place behind the navigation console.

Of course, even there, he wasn't safe from the scrutiny of others. Everyone on the bridge knew Chekov had erred badly. And no one knew that better than Chekov himself.

"Good to see ye back, laddie," Scott said to break the tension. His voice was calm, even friendly.

"Thank you, Mr. Scott" was all the ensign could manage. Chekov ran a quick systems diagnostic and then studied the course and setting.

"Ye missed the fireworks. The rogues got away, but we'll engage them again, no doubt."

"Aye, sir."

Time passed. The chronometer moved with aching slowness. With the starship moving at warp three, there was little for Chekov to do from his post. He would have to remain alert, in case sensors discovered the attackers' ships, but until then, it was business as usual.

Scott stood up from the center seat and moved over to the engineering station. As the chief engineer's fingers flew across the console, Chekov saw Scott scrutinizing the readouts on the highest screen above him. Looking down at the console again, the engineer touched two more buttons and then watched the screen shift color. Harrumphing a bit, he walked back to the center of the bridge and stood right near the ensign.

"I still canna figure out the power curve on those beasties. They move faster than they should and turn like figure skaters, not hunks of tin. What do you think of that?"

Chekov realized Scott was trying to help him. Gratefully he concentrated, running options through his mind as fast as possible.

And then it came to him. "Ve could use the sensor readings to program simulations, study vhat it vas they vere doing," Chekov offered.

"Ah, that we could. Come, give a hand, eh?"

For the next half-hour, the two men worked at their

respective stations, Chekov at the science post and Scott at engineering. They didn't have to say much to each other, but Chekov certainly felt glad to make a contribution.

At last, the study done, Scott walked over and clapped a hand on Chekov's right shoulder. "That's the answer, laddie. They can maneuver far better than we can, making it seem as if they're more powerful. Tricky but not invincible."

"Yes, sir," Chekov acknowledged and smiled. "Thank you for letting me help," he said in a very quiet voice.

"Say nae more about it. Now, shift's over. Go get some rest. I'll bring this up at the staff meeting. The captain's left ye out of it again, but I'll let 'im know ye helped. Might make things easier the next time ye're together up here."

"Thank you, again, Meester Scott. I mean it." Chekov stood, straightened his gold shirt, and left the bridge, feeling like a competent officer for the first time in days.

But no sooner had he entered the turbolift than his spirits fell again. The captain had left him out of a key briefing—again—and might even replace him on the duty roster with another navigator.

Left out of the flow, he reasoned, he might just end his career on the *Enterprise*. Inexorably he fell back into his funk. It was getting to be a familiar place, given how much time he'd spent there of late.

"My name is Dab."

The procreator looked nowhere near as imposing as Endris had. Her eyes were small and black, but that was where the resemblance ended. While the governor was tall and slender, Dab was short and squat, with exaggerated musculature in the area of her hips. Where Endris's crest was high and feathery, the procreator's was short and stiff-looking, almost spiny.

There was another difference as well: the pitch of Dab's voice. Uhura knew from her studies that each caste sounded different; the builders had the deepest voices and the procreators the highest.

"Greetings, Dab. I'm Commodore Robert Wesley, commanding the *Lexington*." A pause, giving Uhura time to complement his speech with her gestures. "How can I be of service to you?"

The procreator seemed hesitant. "Before I answer your question, I must tell you this: it is not customary for those of my caste to speak directly with those of other races. In fact, it has always been our right to speak with anyone we pleased, but it was a right we never exercised, trusting to the governors to embrace our best interests."

Her signing was not as fluid as Endris's, nor as eloquent. But Uhura found it easier to understand.

"We do not feel," Dab went on, "that the governors are embracing our best interests in the present instance. The procreation center must be protected; for our caste, that is of paramount importance."

Wesley glanced at Uhura. "Lieutenant?"

Uhura took a deep breath. "She wants us to remain here, Commodore. That's very clear. She wants us to stay and help—despite the decision of the governors."

Wesley considered the Rithrim on the viewscreen.

"Tell me, Dab. How much authority do you have in this matter?"

"I have sufficient authority," she said.

"An understatement," Uhura noted, interpreting Dab's hand signals. "She has as much authority as Endris, though she seldom uses it."

"You mean we can stay on her say-so?" asked Dr. Coss. "And finish our job at Girin Gatha?"

Uhura looked at him. "According to Dab, yes."

"Of course," Wesley told the procreator, "we'll have to confirm this with the present-cycle governor. But if he doesn't object, we'd be only too glad to follow through on our promise of help."

"That will be appreciated," said Dab. And the viewscreen went blank.

"Well, I'll be damned," muttered the commodore. "Mr. Baila, put me in touch with Mr. Samuels."

The first officer's robust voice seemed to fill the bridge. "We're almost packed up, Commodore."

"Well, *unpack,* Mr. Samuels. There's been a change of plans."

"Sir?"

"You heard me. We just received word from the procreators—and *they* want us to *stay.* I've still got to clear it with Endris, but I don't expect any trouble there."

Samuels grunted. "We'll start setting up again, sir. That'll probably go pretty quickly, too. You get better at these things with practice."

The commodore chuckled. "No doubt you do. Wesley out."

"Sir?" said Uhura.

145

Wesley turned to her. "Yes, Lieutenant?"

"I'd still like to know why the governors changed their minds. And I'd like permission to explore that issue with the procreators."

The commodore mulled it over. "I don't see why not," he replied at last. "After all, they've opened the lines of communication with their caste. You want to try this alone?"

Uhura found her gaze drawn to the communications officer. "Perhaps Mr. Baila could accompany me."

If Wesley was surprised, he concealed it. "Very well, Lieutenant. You've got my blessing. But be careful. I don't want the procreators to change their minds on us the way the governors did."

"I'll keep that in mind, sir," she assured him.

Kirk lay back on his bunk, his hands behind his head, staring up at the ceiling. The ceiling, he noted, never seemed to give him answers to anything. But that was why human beings commanded starships.

At the moment, the *Enterprise* was cruising the Gamma Xaridian system like a shark, moving from one end to the other, as if daring the raiders to return. The crew members might very well have been wasting their time.

While the *Enterprise* patrolled Gamma Xaridian, the raiders might return to Alpha or Beta . . . or anyplace else, for that matter. But if the *Enterprise* went to one of the other systems and the raiders returned to Gamma . . .

Kirk rubbed his temples. That was the sort of

second-guessing that could make someone absolutely crazy.

He was so distracted that at first he didn't hear the beeping of his door. Finally he looked up. "Come," he said.

He expected it to be either Spock or McCoy; anyone else would have used the communications system. As the door hissed open, Kirk smiled at the sight of his first officer. He liked the idea that he knew his crew so well.

"Something, Spock?" Kirk prompted.

The Vulcan sat in the chair opposite Kirk's Spartan desk. In his lap rested a data padd and stylus, and he looked up with a gravity that forced Kirk to pay strict attention.

"Yes, sir. It seems that the Xaridian colonies—"

"The colonies? I thought you were studying the marauder ships," the captain said with surprise in his voice.

"I was, yes. But when further study in that area proved less than fruitful, logic suggested I turn my attention to the colonies." He paused. If Kirk hadn't known better, he'd have said it was for dramatic effect. "When I got to Alpha Xaridian Two—"

"The first colony we visited," said Kirk.

"Yes, sir. I was going over a list, supplied to us by the colony, of materials and machinery that were destroyed . . . and presumed destroyed."

The way Spock hung on those last few words caused Kirk's ears to pick up just slightly. *"Presumed destroyed?"*

"Aye, sir." Spock paused. "At first I was concentrating only on those materials and machines that were found. But I began to notice that certain categories of scientific instrumentation were missing from the debris—all state-of-the-art and unobtainable outside the Federation."

The captain thought about it. "Are you suggesting that the attacks were . . . distractions, Spock? A way for the raiders to beam down scavenger crews and acquire certain technologies?"

The Vulcan nodded. "Perhaps not in all cases; none of the other colonies have reported any loss of equipment. On those worlds random destruction was apparently the raiders' sole motivation. But on this colony, at least, I believe you are correct: theft was a motive behind the attack."

Kirk muttered a curse. "Someone killed thousands for a . . . a shopping list?" He shook his head, feeling the anger build up inside him.

"That is perhaps a simplified description of the events, sir, but an accurate one nonetheless. What is more, the missing equipment would allow a person or persons to construct some of our most advanced machines."

"Which ones, Spock?"

The first officer picked up the padd, took a glance at one of his notations, and then placed it carefully on the edge of Kirk's desk. For Spock, this act of familiarity was a subtle sign of his comfort around Kirk, a comfort he seldom displayed with other humans.

"A complete catalog can be prepared for you, sir, but dozens of items can be built. If we knew who the raiders were, we could more accurately surmise the intent behind the theft of the machinery."

"All right," Kirk said. He flicked a switch to clear his computer screen, then swiveled in his chair. Spock always brought out his sharpest thinking, just another of the many reasons Kirk appreciated the Vulcan so much. "Let's go about this a different way. The equipment is all Federation-issue, which means that member worlds are not now under suspicion. These small ships can't have much in the way of fuel support, so they have a limited range. Could we use the Xaridian system as the center of a search pattern and, from there, make a few educated guesses as to which worlds might be under suspicion?"

Spock nodded. "Of course, Captain. I suggest we assign this task to one of our navigators, since I would like to continue my research into the raiders' weaponry. It might make a difference when we encounter them again."

"Of course. Who's at the top of the duty roster?"

"Ensign Chekov, sir . . . unless you wish him removed."

Kirk paused to consider. He had recently reread Chekov's file and was giving his newest ensign a lot of thought.

Spock must have noticed the captain's hesitation, because he had quietly raised an eyebrow in lieu of repeating his question.

"He froze on the bridge," Kirk explained. "He suggested maneuvers rather than carrying out my order. I don't know if I can trust him during this mission." The captain paused and swiveled around in his chair, regarding his first officer eye to eye. "What do *you* make of Chekov, Spock?"

Steepling his fingers, the Vulcan looked pensive. "I

find his work quite good, and he is a most efficient navigator. In fact, compared with other navigators since you took command of the *Enterprise,* he has displayed a range of skills that is most admirable. He seems to hold his homeland in high regard." A pause. "He is, of course, young; his enthusiasm can get in the way."

Kirk swiveled again and called up Chekov's file on the desktop computer. He took a moment to scan it.

"McCoy apparently thinks that Chekov's love of Mother Russia is a defense mechanism—a way to handle being thrown in with older, more experienced people. I can sympathize with that. The *Enterprise* can be pretty hard on a newcomer."

"I agree, sir," Spock said quietly.

Kirk looked up, suddenly aware of the sensitive area he had casually opened up. "Of course you do, Spock." Kirk frowned. "Do you think he can handle the pressure?"

"On his previous landing-party missions, especially Sharikan and Beta Damoron Five, Chekov served quite well, as you are no doubt aware," Spock began. "His natural curiosity has stood him in good stead at the science station." He shrugged. "I believe he has shown poise under tension. He may make a fine officer in the future."

Kirk nodded and looked away. The Vulcan sat and watched. After nearly a minute of thought, Kirk turned in his chair and nodded. "Okay, Spock, let's give him another chance. Have him research the sector, and let's see what he can do. But if we go to red alert, I want another navigator ready in case he does *not* have what it takes."

"Understood, sir." Spock stood and collected his padd. He turned and walked out, leaving Kirk to study Chekov's file on the computer once again.

Chekov felt more nervous than ever on the bridge, although everything was proceeding smoothly. He had been called back to duty by Spock himself and given a thorough briefing as to what they needed to find.

The ensign was surprised, of course; he'd thought for sure that the captain wouldn't ever trust him again. But here he was, running astrogation maps on the colonies and beginning to work with the theoretical limits of the raiders' ships, as provided by Mr. Scott.

Sulu sat beside him, as effervescent as always. Some of his cheerfulness was finally beginning to rub off on Chekov, who loved working this way.

Spock was in command, but he contented himself with sitting at the science station and conducting further studies on the attackers. Crew came and left; the time seemed to fly by. Finally Chekov was feeling more like a functional part of the crew again.

"Have you found anything yet, Chekov?" Sulu asked.

"No, sir. Mr. Scott thought that the ships would be capable of a four- or five-parsec range, and that's a lot of space to study. But I have figured out that, given the colony location, it is not the Klingons. For that I am grateful."

"Me too," Sulu replied. "We've dealt with them once too often for my taste."

"Aye. But . . . vait a moment. . . . " Chekov trailed

off. He ran his fingers over one of his control panels and then studied the small screen on his left. Once again his fingers flew, rapidly depressing switches. The telltales flickered in a variety of colors. At last, looking over his right shoulder, he beckoned Mr. Spock.

"What have you found, Ensign?" The first officer stepped down to Chekov's station and looked at the screen.

"The attackers may have come from some five or six populated solar systems that we know about, Mr. Spock. But that range also includes Parathu'ul. Didn't they try to gain admission into the Federation?"

"Indeed." Without another word, Spock returned to his science station and began working with the library computer.

Chekov looked to Sulu. The helmsman just shrugged.

A moment later the Russian noted that Spock's computer had been linked to his own station. He watched in fascination as the Vulcan worked the computer like a master chef in his private kitchen.

"Fascinating." Spock stood and looked out at the bridge viewscreen. Then he toggled a switch and called out, "Spock to captain."

Within seconds the screen over the science station snapped on with Kirk's image. He must have been resting; his uniform shirt and his hair were a bit rumpled.

"Yes, Mr. Spock. Have you found something?"

"Actually, Ensign Chekov found something. He pointed out that one of the worlds the raiders may have come from is Parathu'ul."

"But we know what their ship configurations are

like . . . what kind of energy resources they have. You ruled them out some time back."

"Yes. And I still believe they are not the raiders. However, when Mr. Chekov reminded me that they once tried to gain admission to the Federation, I reviewed their original application."

As Chekov watched, Spock seemed to bend closer to the captain's image. "They asked for some of the very same components that are now missing from the colony worlds."

"That still doesn't explain—"

"Mercenaries!"

Chekov had blurted out the word before he knew it. He half expected a reprimand, but instead, Spock nodded. "That would be my inference as well, Ensign." He turned again to the captain. "And once they gain the stolen equipment, they could do what they originally intended: build advanced weapons, which they could use to completely subjugate the rebellious elements in their society."

"I see," Kirk said. "It would seem, Mr. Spock—"

"That a visit to Parathu'ul is in order?" the Vulcan responded.

"Exactly," said the captain. "Kirk out."

No sooner had the captain's voice faded than Sulu leaned over and smiled broadly.

"I think you're out of the doghouse."

"Why?"

"Didn't you hear the captain?"

"All he said was 'I see.' Hardly the kind of praise that would signify being out of the doghouse."

"It wasn't what he said," Sulu explained, "so much as the way he said it."

Chekov shook his head, not taking his eyes off the screen. "We'll see how much trust he has in me when we find the raiders."

"You Russians are certainly good at brooding," Sulu said good-naturedly.

"Ve inwented brooding," the ensign replied solemnly.

Chapter Ten

WHY *HAD* THE GOVERNORS changed their minds about getting involved with the Federation? Wesley leaned back in his command chair and turned the question around in his mind, much as a jeweler would inspect a precious stone.

But it got him no closer to an answer. He didn't know enough about the workings of the Rithramen mind to even venture a guess.

Maybe Uhura would have some luck down at Girin Gatha. She had a good head on her shoulders, and she seemed to enjoy a rapport with the natives. If anyone could—

"Commodore?"

Rousing himself from his reverie, Wesley turned to the junior officer at the communications station. "Yes, Mr. Ling?"

"Sir, I have a subspace packet from Starfleet Command. A mission report they thought you should see."

"Unrestricted access?" asked the commodore.

"Aye, sir, unrestricted."

"Then put it on screen, Mr. Ling."

A moment later Jim Kirk appeared on the forward viewscreen. Wesley smiled at the surprise. Tempted to say something clever, he had to remind himself that this was a recording and not the genuine article.

"This is Captain James T. Kirk of the *Enterprise*," the message began. Kirk looked serious—very serious.

Not going too well, is it, Jim?

"In accordance with my orders, I'm keeping you abreast of what's happening here in the Xaridian systems. Naturally you'll want to relay this to all ships in the vicinity." Kirk paused. "First off, we've engaged the raiders, but without satisfactory results. At one point we managed to separate one of them from the fleet, but it blew itself up rather than be captured by us." A pause. "My chief engineer calls them 'warriors born.' It's an apt description. 'Bloody murderers' would be another."

The commodore grunted softly. Nasty customers. But then, they'd expected them to be.

"Unfortunately," Kirk went on, "we haven't yet found a way to track the raiders, nor do we have any idea how to beat them if we *do* find them. But just recently my staff came up with a theory as to what their motive may be."

Wesley leaned forward in his chair. *This* he wanted to hear.

"Apparently certain materials and machinery were missing from the Alpha Xaridian Two colony site. At first we thought they'd just been destroyed, but now we think otherwise. It turns out that the list of missing materials matches the wish list of a race called the Parath'aa, which applied for Federation membership not so long ago—unsuccessfully, I might add. You can get more on them from your ship's computers, but I can tell you this: their civil rights policies would make even Colonel Green lose his lunch. These people are the last ones I'd want poring over the pride of Federation technology."

The Parath'aa? How interesting, the commodore mused.

"Of course, Parathu'ul isn't generally known for its military prowess. The only logical conclusion is that its leaders have hired mercenaries to do their dirty work."

On the screen Kirk's features hardened. "We're on our way to Parathu'ul now to see if we can prove its link to the raiders. If we're lucky, we'll accomplish more than that—maybe even find a way to stop these killers. If not"—he shrugged—"we could always pull out the old Ouija board. Kirk out."

Wesley smiled grimly. Ouija board indeed. He knew Jim Kirk; quips like that one were his way of letting off steam. The fact that he'd included it in a message to Starfleet Command was an indication of how thoroughly frustrated he was.

What's more, the commodore didn't blame him. In Kirk's place, he'd have been pretty frustrated too. Hell, he was frustrated just from hearing about it.

As he thought this, the screen reverted to an image of Rithra. Wesley sighed. Good luck, Jim, he said silently.

"That's the end of the message," his comm officer reported.

"Yes, Mr. Ling, I noticed. Acknowledge our receipt of the packet."

"Aye, sir."

The commodore made a mental note to apprise Samuels, Uhura, and Baila of the *Enterprise*'s situation. Especially Uhura. She'd want to know how her *old* ship was doing.

"My God," said Baila, peering through his visor at the flood of red-hot lava on the other side of the invisible barrier. He glanced seaward at the clouds of steam. Again: "My God."

Uhura smiled. "I know. It kind of leaves you speechless, doesn't it?"

He nodded. "Yes. Yes, it does."

On the other side of the humped front lawn Samuels was directing the reassembly of the shield generators. But the first officer hadn't taken note of her and Baila, and Uhura could think of no reason to disturb him.

Taking Baila's arm, she turned him in the direction of the procreation center. "Come on. Let's see if we can't get Dab to talk to us."

He wiped his forehead and turned to her. "Tell me the truth, Lieutenant. Why did you bring me along? I mean, it's you who speaks their language. You're the one they're most likely to open up to."

She shrugged. "Haven't you heard? Two heads are better than one."

Baila looked at her through his visor, his eyes full of suspicion. "That's not the reason."

"No? Then what is it?"

"I don't know. Trying to build me up, maybe, in the commodore's eyes?"

"Or maybe in your own?" she returned.

He muttered something and walked past her, headed for the procreation building. "I wasn't looking for pity when I confided in you, Lieutenant."

She caught up to him. "Who said anything about pity? I just want you to see your own worth—to see that you've made yourself into something, despite what your family may think."

Baila frowned, his black eyes smoldering in the red light of the lava flow. "Made myself into what? A failure?"

"A communications officer on a Constitution-class ship, serving under one of the best skippers in the fleet. Last I heard, that was nothing to sneeze at."

"I don't think Wesley would say I'm so terrific."

"I think Wesley would say you *could* be—if you'd stop holding yourself back." She grabbed him by the shoulder and spun him around. "Damn it, Baila, your family was wrong to say the things they did. *Terribly* wrong. Just because *they've* given their souls to Beccah Talulu doesn't mean they can give her *yours!*"

He looked at her, not with anger, but like a child. His brow was beaded with perspiration. "What are you saying?"

She touched his shoulder again, this time more gently. "Can't you see, my friend? It's not you who's dead—it's *them*. Put them past you now, *amuntu*. Be a *man*."

Baila took a deep breath, expelled it. "Be a man," he echoed.

Uhura nodded.

Something seemed to rise up within him, as if his spirit were reawakening, sloughing off the bonds of guilt and self-doubt. It was so obvious a change that Uhura caught her breath.

Maybe that was all Baila had needed: someone to set him straight.

Of course he had a long road back. But the Asians weren't the only ones who had a saying about that first step; the Bantu had philosophers, too.

Baila shook his head. "Blazes, woman, you're something—you know that? Now I know why they call you Freedom."

Uhura smiled.

The doors to the procreation center slid open at their approach, revealing a foyer that was stark and unadorned, illuminated by lighting fixtures set in a double helix pattern in the ceiling. But as Uhura led Baila inside, what struck her more than anything else was the quiet.

Not that it was completely soundless; she could hear the clack of their footfalls on the stone floor and the distant cacophony of tiny voices that reminded her the place was a nursery. But compared to what was going on outside, the procreation center was silence itself. And that was fine with the *Enterprise*'s communications officer, who'd had her fill of the sizzling din during her first visit to Girin Gatha.

There was no one there to greet them, not that Uhura had necessarily expected there would be. However, the corridors that projected from the foyer were bound to be populated with caregivers for the Rithramen young.

Baila looked at her. "Think we'll offend anyone if we go inside?"

Uhura shrugged. "Not if we're discreet about it."

He pointed to the central corridor. "How about this one?"

"Looks as promising as any other," she said.

Together they set off down the hallway in search of a guide. They hadn't gone very far before they passed a nursery window.

It was set up much like a nursery in a hospital back on Earth. Uhura almost expected to see a crowd of parents and well-wishers crowding around to see the new arrivals.

Of course the babies inside didn't look the least bit human. They were too pink, their eyes were too small, and no son of Earth ever had a crest on his head the way these Rithrim did.

"Wonder which caste they are," Baila commented.

Uhura listened to their wailing, muted by the transparent wall between them and the infants. "Gatherers," she concluded.

Her companion looked at her. "How can you tell?" And then, before she could reply, he came up with the answer himself: "That's right. By the pitch of their voices."

Among the Rithrim, pitch was established at birth, even if other physical characteristics were not. It was nature's way of ensuring that infants would be caste-identified and segregated immediately so that their caste specialty could be honed.

Peering through the nursery window, Baila shook his head. "Isn't it funny? When you listen closely, they sound like adults instead of babies."

"It is funny," she conceded.

"May I help you?" said a voice directly behind them.

Uhura whirled and saw a procreator with her hands clasped against her chest. They'd been so enthralled with the young that they hadn't heard her approach.

"I hope so," she told the Rithrim, as she did her best to recover from her surprise. "We're looking for Dab."

"Dab?" the procreator repeated. And then: "I can lead you to her, but . . ."

"Is there a problem?" asked Uhura. "We just spoke with her a little while ago, when we were up on our ship."

The Rithrim seemed to think for a moment. Finally she indicated with her hands that she'd come to a conclusion, if an uncertain one.

"No," she said. "No problem. Come with me, please."

They followed the procreator down the corridor. Before they'd gone fifty paces, they'd passed two other nurseries: one for baby builders and the other for newborn governors.

There was only one more window between them and the door. Like all the others, this nursery was full, every berth filled with a bawling infant.

Just out of curiosity Uhura listened for their pitch. Judging by the tilt of his head, Baila was listening, too.

But there was something strange here. The babies were howling at a pitch she didn't recognize.

Stopping, Uhura listened more intently, just to be sure. However, she'd been right the first time. The pitch was off—not just in one or two of the babies but in all of them.

Baila had stopped also. He regarded her. "You hear it also?"

She nodded. "And I've got a good ear for such things."

The procreator looked up at them. "Something is amiss?" she asked.

"Not really," Uhura assured her. "We were just wondering about these babies. Their voices are too low-pitched to be governors and too high-pitched to be gatherers."

The procreator looked at them helplessly. "I do not understand your question." Her hands were absolutely silent—a very unusual condition for a Rithrim. "Perhaps Dab can answer it."

Uhura nodded. "Perhaps."

Obviously eager to get going, the procreator hurried through the door, barely giving it time to slide away. Exchanging glances, the Starfleet officers followed her through.

Silva, the planetary leader of Parathu'ul, smiled thinly, which of course was the only way he *could* smile. He steepled his long, slender fingers and glanced around the room at his visitors, who were saying nothing.

"You are being joking with me, yes?" he asked politely.

"We are being joking with you, no," replied Kirk. Spock stood next to Kirk, largely for effect. Kirk had noticed that the mere presence of the forbidding, inscrutable Vulcan was enough to unnerve anyone being questioned about a transgression.

Apparently, however, the Parath'aa were able to suppress their terror. Silva even made a sound that resembled a soft chuckle. "This is being quite a surprise, Captain. Here we're being open and honest about our knowledge of these raiders, which admittedly is minimal. And now you are being accusatory of us. Saying that we are somehow not only aware of their identities, but are supportive of them, or even their employers."

"The thought had occurred to us," said Kirk.

Silva sighed and shook his head. "Such disappointment we are feeling now, Captain. Such sadness. Here we are being hopeful of joining the Federation, and you act in this manner."

"I find it an interesting coincidence," said Kirk, "that your petition to join the Federation came very, very shortly after the raiders started their attacks in this system. One could argue the remarkable timing. On the one hand, you could be pursuing your desire for technology through means of conquest, while on the other hand you try to throw suspicion away from yourselves by approaching the Federation on peaceful terms."

"Intriguing the way in which your mind works, Captain," said Silva calmly. He rose and looked out his window, gazing across the great square. "Now as for myself, I would be pointing out that the presence of the raiders might simply serve to underscore what a dangerous place the galaxy can be and how important it is being to have friends and protection. Is that not as reasonable an explanation for events as your own? What do you think, Mr. Spock?"

"It is not unreasonable," Spock said carefully.

"There!" Silva said triumphantly. "It is not being unreasonable. Of what higher vindication can we be hoping than that of a Vulcan."

Kirk shot a look at his first officer, who merely looked back impassively. "It is not unreasonable, Captain," Spock said again.

"Besides," Silva added, "there is not being absolutely conclusive proof that any equipment or materials is being missing from Alpha Xaridian Two. In fact, as you have yourselves being telling us, other attacked worlds have not been robbed at all. Destruction, yes. Terrible destruction"—he shuddered slightly in sympathy—"but not theft. Now, why would raiders being stealing on one world and not on others? Other worlds have other technology that we Parath'aa would like. Why are they not being looted?"

"Yes, I was thinking about that very thing myself," said Kirk. "I've been giving that a lot of thought. And you know what I've come up with?"

Silva shook his head politely.

"ABC murders," said Kirk.

At that, Silva looked utterly confused. He looked to his compatriots for an explanation, but none was forthcoming. "I'm sorry?"

"It's a method of murdering someone and disguising your motive," said Kirk. "Let's say that you want to murder Person A. But you're afraid that this action will inevitably point to you as the murderer, since anyone who might want Person A murdered would doubtless be investigated."

"Oh, doubtless," confirmed Silva, still not entirely following.

"So you murder Person A, and not too long afterward, you murder Person B. And then Person C, D, E, and so on. You do so using some very obvious pattern that the authorities are certain to notice. That way they will falsely conclude that they are dealing with some sort of pattern serial killer rather than with someone who really wanted only one person dead but went to great trouble to cover his tracks."

"I do not fully understand the parallel," said Silva.

Kirk walked slowly toward him and stopped barely a foot away. "Oh, I think you do," he said. "The attackers get much, if not all, of what they need on the first colony world they attack. But they don't want it to be obvious that they're stealing technology which might be connected with you. So they attack other colonies, focusing purely on the devastation so that they'll be perceived as engines of destruction rather than thieves. And they continue on this course until they, and you, are convinced that the trail toward you is ice cold. Am I making myself clear enough now, Silva?"

Silva's body seemed to tremble for a moment, and then in a low and deadly voice, he said, "Captain . . . we are being polite hosts. But you are being rude visitor. We will be asking you to leave."

Kirk glared at him through narrowed eyes and waited for the Parath'aa leader to crack. Unfortunately this technique didn't meet with much more success than the strategy of bringing a Vulcan with him. The Parath'aa were, apparently, unflappable.

His gaze never leaving the Parath'aa, Kirk flipped

open his communicator. "Kirk to *Enterprise*. Two to beam up." He closed the device and said quietly, "We'll be keeping an eye on you, Silva."

"Enjoy the view, Captain Kirk" was Silva's calm reply.

When Kirk and Spock stepped off the transporter pads, McCoy was waiting for them. "Well? How did it go?"

"They broke down completely and threw themselves on our mercy," Kirk informed him.

"Hunh. Didn't admit to a thing, did they?"

"Not a thing."

The wall communicator sounded, and Palmer's voice came down. "Bridge to captain."

From the tone of her voice, Kirk already had a hunch what this call was going to be about. He walked quickly to the wall unit and punched a button. "Kirk here. Who's being attacked now?"

Palmer did not even hesitate despite Kirk's small display of telepathy. "Beta Xaridian Four."

"Lay in a course. Inform Engineering I'll need warp eight. This time there are no ships buying us additional time. I'm on my way up." He clicked off and turned to Spock. "It would appear," he said as they headed out of the transporter room, "that Administrator Jarvis and the colonists of Beta Xaridian Four have just watched their luck run out. I hope to God we get there in time to restore it."

Chapter Eleven

DAB'S OFFICE, if it could be called that, was a large room in which one entire wall was composed of viewscreens—sixteen of them, each showing a different nursery.

"I was not informed of your coming," said the head of the procreator caste.

"Our apologies," Uhura told her. Her hand movements echoed her words. "I regret any inconvenience we may have caused."

Dab eyed them. "It is no inconvenience"—especially in light of the help the *Lexington* is giving the procreation center, she added in sign language.

"As you may have noticed," Baila said, "our engineers have begun reassembling their shield projectors."

Dab nodded. "I have indeed noticed." Her hands asked: How long before the shields will start working?

"They should be up and running in three to four days," said Uhura. "That's what I'm told by Mr. Samuels, who is in charge of the operation." She used signs to indicate that four days would be the maximum.

"That is good." The procreator indicated her approval. "Some of the offspring we nurture here have gotten sickly in recent days. Your assistance has come none too soon."

For a moment there was silence. Uhura considered the best way of bringing up the governors' sudden change of heart and finally decided that the direct approach might be the most useful.

"Procreator Dab," she began, "we've been unable to fathom the governors' reasons for changing their minds about our helping you here. We certainly don't mean to pry into anything that's not our business, but we believe that the better we understand Rithrim of all castes, the more helpful we can be to you."

Dab nodded. "Your request is a reasonable one. What is more, I have some inkling of the governors' thinking on the subject, even if I disagree with it." She paused. "However, I cannot divulge the information you seek. Only the governors may provide it."

Uhura didn't like getting stonewalled—but she didn't say so. What she said was "Thank you for your honesty, Procreator Dab."

"You are quite welcome." Dab sat back in her chair. "If our business is concluded here," she told them, "various matters await my attention." Her hands were already bidding her visitors farewell, figuratively ushering them out the door.

"Actually," said Baila, "there is one other thing. Nothing important—just a matter of curiosity."

"Ask," the procreator instructed him. "I will answer if I may."

The communications officer licked his lips. "Outside, in the hallway, we came upon a caste nursery we had trouble identifying."

"Oh?"

"That's right," Uhura chimed in. "The pitch of the babies' voices is different from that of any of the four castes."

Dab shook her head. "You must be mistaken. There are only four pitches; the pitch in the nursery you speak of must be one of the four."

Her hands were immobile—just like those of the procreator they'd encountered in the corridor. Uhura noted the fact and wondered about it.

Baila must have noticed, too, because he didn't press the issue. He just inclined his head to the procreator.

"Perhaps we were mistaken," he said. "Thank you for your indulgence."

"Again, you are welcome." Dab pressed a button on her desk, and a moment later another procreator came in—though it didn't seem to be the one who had led them to this office.

"See to it that our visitors are escorted out," instructed Dab. Her hand signals made the order into a request.

"Gladly," said the newcomer. She signed to the humans. "Come with me."

And so they left Dab's office—albeit with more questions than they'd had when they entered.

The damage reports were coming in fast and furiously to the emergency command center where Administrator Sharon Jarvis and her closest aides had secured themselves. Bunkers had been hollowed out below the ground and lined with duranium, affording the cowering colonists a sizable degree of protection. Overhead Jarvis could hear the pounding of the raiders' weapons, the roar of their ships, as the deadly vessels strafed the surface of the planet looking for new targets.

One of her aides, Joan Winston, had a small communicator pressed against her ear. She called out to Jarvis, "Ground defense crews are keeping the raiders hopping! Our securing the crews against mountainsides has given them added shelter . . . at least for the moment."

"Come on, Kirk," breathed Jarvis. "What are you waiting for, an engraved invitation? Get your interstellar ass over here."

"Coming up on Beta Xaridian Four, Captain," Sulu said, as the *Enterprise* dropped out of warp speed. "We'll be in range within two minutes."

"Red alert. Raise shields. All hailing frequencies," said Kirk, experiencing a natural feeling of déjà vu. By all reason, there was no need to go through the pretense that the raiders were going to be interested in chatting.

The call came up from Engineering. "Captain, you can't be thinking of taking us into battle again so soon?" came the voice of the chief engineer, bordering on indignation.

"It had crossed my mind, Mr. Scott. We'll need everything you've got."

"Captain," Scotty said in horror, "I'll need another three hours to fully restore all systems! As it is, she's being held together with spit and bailing wire!"

There was one thing to be said for Scotty, the captain mused: the engineer did not waste a great deal of time recounting technical details. He had once commented that it wasn't necessary to "waste the captain's time with such trivia," but Kirk suspected that Scott simply assumed the details would be too complicated for Kirk to understand.

"In that case, Mr. Scott, I suggest you work up some more spit."

"Aye, sir," Scotty said wearily. Clearly he was not happy with the way things were working out.

"Sensors indicate power expenditures near the planet surface," Spock announced. "It would appear that the raiders have already begun their assault. The colonists are defending themselves adequately, but they cannot hold out forever."

Somewhere below the atmosphere, where the *Enterprise* could not go, the brazen attackers were assaulting the colonists. Kirk felt a cold fury building in him.

"No response on any channels," Palmer announced.

"If we fire down on the raiders with phasers set on maximum—" Sulu began.

"We risk killing the colonists, and there's no guarantee that we'll hit any of the raiders," finished Kirk. "Perhaps wide-range phaser stun . . ."

"That would most certainly stun the colonists, and

they could not protect themselves," said Spock. "And the shielding of the raiders' ships—although vulnerable enough at close range with direct hits—would seem to be quite formidable at a distance.

Palmer added ruefully, "The likelihood is that they wouldn't even be slowed down."

"Quite correct, Lieutenant."

"Send down shuttles?"

"They would be outmaneuvered and outgunned," said Spock. "It would be suicide."

"We have to bring them to us, damn it!" said Kirk.

Chekov's gaze went from one person to the other as he followed the rapid conversation with wide-eyed amazement. He was impressed with the smoothness with which the crew examined possibilities, analyzing and discarding them. And it occurred to him that frequently such analyses went on right inside the captain's head. Silently he would evaluate and select strategies, then order them so smoothly and efficiently that one never suspected the effort that went into the decision.

And when the captain needed suggestions, the bridge crew served as extensions of his own mind. They verbalized the options that he might already be reviewing, or that had not occurred to him. All of the discussion centered around the captain, and in turn he affected every part of the bridge. The steady flow of information, delivered by trained professionals, was dazzling and impressive.

Chekov opened his mouth as a fleeting thought occurred to him. But he still felt abashed and confused over the earlier business that had cost him—for however brief a time—his valued position on the bridge. He did not want to do anything to risk such a fate befalling him again. So he closed his mouth without voicing his opinion.

The momentary facial expression, however, was not lost on Kirk. And Chekov blanched as he heard Kirk's voice say, "Mr. Chekov . . . you have something to contribute?"

"We have to protect the colonists," said Chekov. "If we protect them, the raiders will come after us."

"Yes, Mr. Chekov," said Kirk impatiently. "Any thoughts as to how we can protect them?"

Chekov glanced desperately at Sulu. The message in the helmsman's eye was clear: If you have an idea, spit it out.

"The colony is only a few miles long," said Chekov. "We could erect shields over it using our deflectors."

"Defensive shielding only covers the ship," Palmer said. "It won't extend all the way down to a planet's surface!"

"Not those deflectors," said Chekov. "The—"

And Kirk sat bolt upright, as if someone had jabbed a cattle prod into his back. "The navigational deflectors!"

"Yes, Captain. Normally they're fully automated, extending miles in front of the ship, shoving aside meteors and debris so they won't strike the ship. But if the navigational deflectors can be recalibrated—"

"Spock!" Kirk was already turning to the Vulcan. "Can you do it?"

Spock was moving before Kirk got halfway through the sentence. In an instant he was standing over Chekov's navigational computer. Chekov started to rise in order to give the Vulcan more room, but Spock gestured him back down with a quick shake of his head. His fingers were already manipulating the computer controls.

"I've taken manual control of the navigational deflectors," Spock said as if talking from a great distance, "and am rerouting them through the main deflector dish while I reconfigure the beam."

The word "trivia" went through Kirk's mind, said with a heavy Scottish burr. "Will it protect the colonists?"

"It will create a barrier fashioned from extremely narrow, but extremely effective, deflector beams spread along the perimeter of the colony and with a pinnacle of"—he checked quickly—"one thousand meters. Sir, the computer instruction is on line."

"Perfect. However, that is the navigation station. The navigator, by rights, should handle the finishing touches. Ensign?"

Chekov nodded as he activated the recalibrated navigational beam.

On the planet's surface one of the raiders was diving straight toward the bunker in which Jarvis and a number of other colonists were secured. The bunker was squarely in the vessel's sights, and a quick flip of a trigger would have been enough to rain destruction down upon them.

The trigger, however, was not flipped, quickly or otherwise, for the deflector beams materialized directly in front of the raider, too close for even the unusually agile ship to avoid. The raider crashed headlong into beams that had been designed to brush aside or pulverize floating space matter. At the speed with which the raider was moving, the deflector became the immovable object against the raider's irresistible force. The object resisted the force without significant difficulty, and the raider exploded into an extremely impressive fireball that skipped along the edge of the conical defensive shield and ended up several miles away.

The other raiders were able to react quickly enough, however, and they veered off from the defense screen in time. They swarmed around it like maddened hornets, firing in frustration.

"They're trying to batter down the navigational deflector beams, sir," reported Sulu.

Kirk looked like a Buddha. "Let them." He punched down to Engineering. "Scotty, I want all power fed into those beams. Reserves. Everything."

The engineer sounded worried, but said simply, "Aye, sir."

Chekov turned in his chair. "You wish to leave us defenseless, Captain?"

"Criticizing, Ensign?"

"Inquiring, Captain."

"Navigational deflectors holding, sir," said Sulu. "Our own shields are fading, but the cone is holding steady on the planet."

Kirk hadn't looked away from Chekov. "We don't need defenses, do we, Ensign?"

Chekov pondered the question for only a moment. "No, sir. Not while they're down there and we're up here."

"Precisely."

"But we can't keep the navigational force shield in place indefinitely," Chekov pointed out.

It was Spock who replied. "They do not know that, Ensign."

"The question will be," said Kirk, "which will have greater limits: our power or their patience."

It didn't take long to learn the answer. "Attacks on the defensive cone have ceased," Spock announced from his hooded station, and then, a moment later: "Raiders approaching at three-two-two mark nine."

"Captain," said Chekov in a determinedly neutral voice. "When they attack, we'll have to shift defenses back to the *Enterprise*. The colony will be unprotected. If they should leave ships behind to continue the assault—"

"They won't," said Kirk.

"But—"

"I said," Kirk repeated with confidence, "they won't."

"Incoming attackers!" called Sulu. "Seven . . . no, eight."

"So that wasn't their entire fleet we encountered before," said Kirk. "Redirect power to ship's deflectors. Mr. Sulu, are any of the raiders still at planet altitude?"

"No, sir, they're all in space."

Kirk smiled. "Mr. Sulu, fire at will. Phasers and photon torpedoes."

The *Enterprise* armament lashed out at the raiders, and once more the ships bobbed and weaved with alacrity. But Sulu was studying them carefully, and even as he fired at what was on the screen, he studied quick replays of their moves across his helm display.

"I'm starting to notice some patterns," said Sulu. "I think I can anticipate some of their moves this time."

"Best guesses, Mr. Sulu. Fire!"

Sulu quickly tracked two of the ships and fired off a phaser blast directly into their path while at the exact same time releasing an array of photon torpedoes into the direction he was certain that the ships would steer.

He was rewarded with partial success. Two of the ships managed to avoid the torpedoes, but two others were not so fortunate. The torpedoes caromed directly into them . . .

And bounced away. The ships were wobbling and off kilter, but otherwise seemed unhurt.

Sulu took advantage of their momentary disorientation to batter them with phaser blasts. But the main battery of the *Enterprise* offense seemed to have as little effect as did the torpedoes—little effect physically, that was.

Psychologically, however, it seemed that the *Enterprise* had given them more than they wished to swallow. The raiders suddenly came together, swept down and around, and shot behind Beta Xaridian IV. The clever positioning put the planet between them and the starship; the only way the *Enterprise* could fire on them was to shoot straight through the planet. That would have been, to put it mildly, counterproductive.

The *Enterprise* whipped around the planet as fast as the impulse engines would drive it, but by that time it was too late. The smaller ships had gone into warp.

"Damn," muttered Kirk.

"They were moving slower," said Sulu. "They were definitely moving slower. Maybe we're wearing them out."

"Let's hope we have the opportunity to wear them out even more," said Kirk. "Lieutenant Palmer, signal Beta Xaridian Four that all is clear. Mr. Chekov, restore the navigational deflector to normal usage. And nice thinking about the use of those navigational deflectors."

Chekov bobbed his head slightly in acknowledgment, then screwed his courage to the sticking place and said, "Captain . . . how did you know they would attack us in full numbers instead of splitting their forces?"

"They'd lost the element of surprise for the planet raid," said Kirk. "If our theory is correct, their goals are more on an as-need basis than graven in stone. They could afford to retreat. What they could not afford was to face the *Enterprise* at less than full strength. If they'd sent half their force up here and left the rest planetside, they would have risked our defeating the smaller number while the remainder were stuck below. They had to face us in as large a number as possible; it was their best chance for accomplishing anything, including the possible destruction of this ship."

"And you knew all that for sure?" said Chekov admiringly.

Kirk sighed. "Mr. Chekov, the first thing they taught us in command school is that the captain can be right or the captain can be wrong, but the one thing the captain cannot be . . . is unsure." He paused and then added, "Even if he doesn't have a clue."

Chapter Twelve

WESLEY LEANED BACK in his chair, surveying the two communications officers across his conference room table. "Maybe you *were* mistaken," he suggested.

Uhura shook her head. "No chance, sir. I've got perfect pitch."

"Dab and her people are lying," insisted Baila. "There's something about that nursery they don't want us to know about."

Uhura nodded. "I could tell by their hands—they weren't moving them when they discussed the nursery. I'll bet it's easier for them to deceive with the spoken word than with their sign language."

Wesley digested the information. "All right. Let's say for the moment that they're lying. What does it mean?"

Uhura frowned. What indeed?

"Could it be," Baila suggested, "that there's a connection between the mystery nursery and the missing statues?"

That roused the commodore's interest. "Could be," he replied. "Care to venture a theory, Lieutenant?"

Uhura heard the challenge in Wesley's words, even if Baila didn't. The commodore was daring the man to make a real contribution—to prove his worth.

Baila thought for a moment. Finally he shook his head. "No, sir. No th—" Suddenly, his eyes lit up. "I take that back," he said. "I *have* got a theory. And it's a whopper."

Uhura leaned forward. "Well? Don't leave us in suspense."

"How about this: What if there are *more* than four castes in Rithramen society? What if there are *five?*"

"Five?" Uhura echoed, starting to see the possibilities even as Baila laid them out.

"That's right, five. But maybe there's something about the fifth caste that makes the other Rithrim want to disown them. Something they did—"

"Or maybe something the other Rithrim did *to* them," Uhura interjected. "Something the other Rithrim weren't very proud of."

Baila's temples worked. "Either way, the fifth caste disappeared somehow. Maybe they were banished to another world; maybe they died. And now the governors and the gatherers and the builders and the procreators are trying to sweep them under the rug."

Wesley's eyes narrowed. "Then the statuary they're destroying . . ."

"Depicts the fifth caste," Baila finished for him.

"But of course they can't obliterate the caste's presence in society altogether. It would still be represented in the gene pool; infants would still be born with fifth-caste characteristics."

Uhura saw where he was going with this. "It makes sense," she remarked. "It makes a whole lot of sense." She turned to the commodore. "The babies in that nursery were definitely not of any caste we know about."

Wesley looked from one to the other of them. "Now that I think about it," he said, "we had just asked Endris about the statuary when he told us we were to leave Rithra. At the time, I thought nothing of it; he made it sound as if the decision had already been made. But now I'm not so sure." He shook his head. "Could they be so ashamed of this fifth caste that they'd sacrifice a procreation center to keep us from the truth?"

"People have sacrificed more for less," Uhura reminded him.

"Maybe you're right, Lieutenant. But what could have happened that was so terrible? All the Rithrim we've met are peaceful to a fault."

"Let's see," said Baila. "Governors. Gatherers. Procreators. Builders." He ticked the castes off on his fingers as he named them. "All the basic functions of a society. What am I leaving out?"

Uhura thought about it. What was the analogy Baila had made early on? He'd compared the Rithrim to . . . Terran insects, right? Right. So what did an insect colony have that Rithramen society didn't? What—

"Oh, my God," said Uhura, without meaning to speak out loud. She looked at Wesley and Baila and saw the stares they were giving her.

"Yes, Lieutenant?" prodded the commodore.

Uhura leaned forward. "I think I've got it, sir."

"It's not working. I'll *never* get it to work."

Overhearing the complaint, Scotty walked outside his office and looked down into the engineering section. He was never quite sure why the architects had decided to put the chief engineer's office atop a ladder, but there it was.

Down below, two engineers huddled over a circuit board. One, a dark-haired man named Washburn, was trying to reattach three small circuits, using tiny tools. The other, a tall, slender black woman named Masters, was overseeing the job with a flashlight.

"Cheer up, Washburn," Masters said gently. "We'll get it fixed. And remember, this is a redundancy system we're repairing. It's not like the warp engines depend on it this instant."

Washburn wiped some sweat from his forehead with the back of his hand. "You're right. I guess I've just been working too hard." He went back to his work, getting it right on the next try.

Scotty couldn't help but notice that all the spirits aboard the *Enterprise* were flagging. Twice now they had encountered these mysterious attackers and twice they had gotten away, but the confrontations were taking their toll.

Surveying the rest of his domain, Scotty watched men and women repair minor damage and reintegrate circuits that had fused. His pride in his personnel and equipment was second to none, probably not even to Kirk's pride in the *Enterprise*.

"Mr. Scott?"

He followed the voice to its source. "Aye, Mr. Stanley?"

"Sir, the dilithium chamber checks out just fine. The power fluctuation you found was from a forward converter."

"Did you repair the problem?"

"All done, sir."

"Good. Then you and Gabler should go down and check the impulse integration relays. We may need to maneuver quickly when we find those beasties again."

Stanley nodded and left the main engine room. Satisfied that things were going as well as could be expected, Scott went back into his office and sat down behind his desk.

Sighing, he took another look at the mission monitor board, a schematic of the *Enterprise* on the rear wall. The controls rested on his desk, allowing him to override just about all the ship's main functions.

Scott studied the status of each system. All signs were green, meaning the ship was ready for just about anything. He paused to listen to the thrum of the engines, and a slow smile spread across his face.

"Warp two," he said softly and then looked at a bridge monitor. Sure enough, they were moving at warp two.

With all as it should be, Scott turned his attention to the raiders again. Their design and maneuverability intrigued him. He accessed the library computer and tied in with his own files of ship design—both those dealing with the practical and those dealing with the theoretical.

While the raiders' exact configuration did not register, Scott noted its similarities to ships from the Orion worlds. He shook his head sadly, thinking about how such fine design was wasted on thieves and slavers.

Scott then asked the computer to display engine readouts that the sensors had managed to record during the two confrontations. The screen lit up to display colorful charts showing engine output.

He was interested to see that the color flow was steady, quite unlike most Federation ship designs. The color charts were encoded with notations on radiation residue, waste, chemical composition, and other details, almost down to the microscopic level. After studying the readouts for a moment, he asked the computer to slow down the playback.

Scott watched intently as the colors slowly shifted from one hue to another, with the accompanying data changing accordingly. He flipped two switches and asked the computer for a closer detailed analysis of the engine section alone.

As the computer complied, Scott snapped on an auxiliary console and ran some separate notations. He could have spoken directly to the computer and had it run the information, but he needed to do something with his hands, and it was always good practice to stay in physical contact with the equipment itself.

The engineering chief ran the information once more. Wait a second. . . .

"Damn!" he exclaimed out loud—and hit the communications panel. "Engineering to Mr. Spock."

"Spock here," came the almost instantaneous reply. Didn't the Vulcan ever sleep?

"I think I've found a way to track the marauders," Scotty said.

"Indeed. Continue, Mr. Scott."

The engineer licked his lips. "Like all engines, the raiders' produce trace ions. But unlike our engines, theirs are negatively charged."

Spock was silent for a moment. "And we can use that fact to follow them to their hiding place. Good work, Mr. Scott. I will inform the captain. Bridge out."

Scotty sat back in his chair and shook his head. He'd just turned the whole bloody mission around— and the only thing Spock could say was "Good work."

Ah, well. Another day, another miracle.

Spock snapped off the communication channel and relayed Scott's discovery to the captain, who was engaged in discussion with Sulu. Kirk's reaction was as expected.

"Terrific, Spock. Mr. Sulu, tie in with full sensor sweeps and find the marauders. As soon as you find something, have Chekov lay in a course. We may *have* something here."

"Aye-aye." Sulu's reply was tinged with excitement.

"You know, Spock," Kirk began, "finding them is only half the battle. We've still got to *beat* them."

"Yes, sir. I am awaiting a final analysis from Lieutenant Commander Giotto on tactical maneuvers. He is replaying the two confrontations and running simulations."

"At least this time we have that luxury," Kirk said.

He looked out at the bridge, noting how all members of the crew set eagerly about their tasks. Scott's good news had come at just the right time.

"Sir?" Spock had taken up a position just behind and to one side of the captain.

Kirk turned to him. "Yes, Spock?"

The Vulcan spoke in a low voice. "You are about to begin your third consecutive shift on the bridge. Is it not time to obtain some rest?"

The captain smiled. Though he hadn't really thought about it, he realized that he *could* use a rest. The last thing he wanted was to have to confront the raiders without his wits about him.

"You win, Spock." Turning to his helmsman, he said, "You have the conn, Mr. Sulu."

"Aye-aye, sir," came the response.

As Kirk got up and headed for the turbolift, he saw the first officer take his place. Fortunately Vulcans could go a lot longer without sleep than humans could.

A moment later he was inside the lift, watching the doors close—but thinking about anything but rest. After all, he'd engaged the mystery fleet twice and barely managed a draw.

What could he do differently the next time? Part of him wanted to ask Starfleet for a backup ship. Maybe a second starship would help—and then again, maybe not. Besides, the nearest vessel was the *Lexington,* and Bob Wesley was busy enough.

No, he'd have to handle this one himself, just as he'd handled other tough missions in the past. He'd rely on his wits, his officers' skills . . . and a little luck.

* * *

The governors' courtyard was every bit as imposing now as it had been the first time Uhura had seen it, and every bit as bright. As before, Uhura materialized alongside Wesley, Baila, Samuels, and Dr. Coss; as before, the governors awaited them on the opposite side of the small blue-green pool.

Of course there were some differences as well. For one thing, the builders were no longer in evidence, apparently having completed their labors. They'd done a good job, too; the fresco they'd been working on was as old- and venerable-looking as any other.

The other difference, and by far the more significant one, was the presence of Dab. As silent as any of Endris's companions, the procreator stood to one side of the governors' bench in a sleeveless white garment.

The present-cycle governor got to his feet. "Welcome," he said.

His hands conveyed a somewhat different message: one that was heavy with urgency. After all, the people from the *Enterprise* had already been asked to leave, hadn't they? What was this meeting about, anyway, and why was it necessary for a procreator, even one as high-placed as Dab, to be there?

All this Endris said with his hands. But Uhura didn't translate; she'd made the commodore aware of the governor's impatience before they beamed down. Judging from Endris's gestures, she was surprised he had agreed to this talk at all.

His attitude didn't bode well for the outcome of this discussion. Wesley had hoped that once the Rithrim's secret was out in the open, they'd agree to let the Federation people stay and help out at Girin Gatha. But Endris's impatience put that hope in jeopardy.

Hell, maybe exposing the Rithrim's secret would make the governors that much *more* determined to kick them out. One never knew.

"Sit," Endris instructed the visitors.

"Actually," said the commodore, "I'd prefer to stand. You see, where I come from, no one sits unless there's a seat for everyone. And I don't see anywhere for Procreator Dab to sit."

Uhura expanded on the idea for the benefit of the Rithrim. It was difficult to get across the very human idea of chivalry, but she managed.

The present-cycle governor hesitated for a moment. Then he said: "There is no slight intended to Procreator Dab—nor, I assure you, does she perceive one. Of course, you may sit or stand as you wish." And he sat.

"Nice start," whispered Coss.

"Thanks for the encouragement," returned Wesley. He cleared his throat. "Governors . . . Procreator Dab . . . I am probably overstepping my bounds with what I am about to say. If I weren't so concerned about the health of your people at Girin Gatha, I wouldn't even consider it." He looked around the courtyard as if admiring the stone-carving work that had gone into it. "This is a beautiful place. An ancient place. And like many ancient places, it hides a secret, doesn't it?"

Uhura looked for the governors' reactions—in their hands. She wasn't disappointed. The Rithrim's fingers were clenched in obvious anxiety. Only Dab seemed relaxed—almost relieved.

"It seems to us," the commodore went on, "that not so long ago, there were *five* castes on this planet. A caste of governors, a caste of builders, a caste of gatherers, a caste of procreators—and a caste of *warriors*. There's no crime in Rithramen society now, no strife, but that couldn't always have been the case. There had to be soldiers, defenders, police—people who could bring force to bear in the protection of your earliest pockets of civilization."

Uhura searched for some sign that they'd guessed wrong. She saw none.

"Bingo?" muttered Baila.

"Bingo," she confirmed.

"But something happened to that fifth caste," said Wesley, gathering steam. "Something that made your society feel ashamed, either of the warrior caste or of itself. So you decided to obliterate them and the memory of them." He indicated the walls of the courtyard with a sweep of his arm. "To wipe out all trace of them, here and elsewhere."

The commodore eyed the governors again. "Maybe when you invited us here, you didn't think we'd notice what you were doing. But we noticed, and we asked about it. And you thought we were getting too close to your secret, so you asked us to leave, choosing to sacrifice the lives of many of your young rather than let us find out what happened to your warrior caste."

Wesley paused. "Well, I'm here to tell you I don't give a damn what happened to them. Sure, I'm curious. But I'm not here to judge you; that's not what the Federation is all about. The only thing of any importance to me is to make sure the procreators and the children are safe at Girin Gatha."

Silence. For a moment no one moved. Then Endris made a distinct and deliberate sign of dismissal.

"You have come to an erroneous conclusion," he

said, perfect calm in his voice. His gestures emphasized the words. "There has never been a fifth caste on Rithra. What is more, we resent your temerity. We were under the impression that when we asked you to leave, you would do so without conducting an investigation."

It was painfully obvious to Uhura that Endris was lying. But there was nothing she could do about it. It was the Rithrim's planet, not theirs.

But Wesley had one more card to play. He turned to Dab, who had been quiet all this time.

"Is this what *you* want, Procreator?"

For what seemed like a long time, Dab returned the commodore's gaze. Finally she spoke—but not to Wesley.

Turning to the governors, she said: "It is over; they know that. And I am glad, because there is no longer any reason to let the little ones die."

If Endris was angry with her, he didn't show it—not even in his hands. Rather, he signified acceptance, even resignation.

Regarding the Federation team anew, the present-cycle governor stood. His black-robed figure was reflected in the still waters of the pool. "You are correct," Endris said. "There is a fifth caste, a warrior caste. And we are indeed pained by the choices they have made."

He paused—though his hands kept going, eloquently expressing the depth of his distress.

"In the old days the warriors were a valued part of our society. They enforced our laws; they prevented us from inflicting harm on one another. Then, when our race matured beyond intraspecific aggression, we turned to the stars, and the fifth caste found another function: the defense of Rithra against the peoples we encountered in space.

"As it happened, we encountered few peoples, and none of them turned out to be a threat. However, that did not prevent the warriors from being prepared. Over the years they honed their instellar battle capabilities to a fine point, becoming acutely skilled pilots and marksmen. But they never got a chance to exercise their skills in battle.

"It was becoming increasingly obvious," Endris explained, "that the warriors no longer had a role on Rithra. Worse, given no other outlet, they began to turn their aggressive instincts on one another. For the first time in centuries there was bloodshed among Rithrim—internecine conflicts between growing factions of warriors. Ironically, sadly, the caste nature had designed to stem violence had become the cause of it."

As Uhura listened to the governor, something gnawed at her. An annoyance, she thought at first, a distraction. She was so intrigued by Endris's words that she tried to dismiss it, to push it aside.

But she couldn't. Because as the governor went on, she realized where he was going with his speech—and that what seemed to be a distraction was just her mind's way of putting two and two together.

Nor was she alone in that, apparently. As she looked at Wesley, Baila, Coss, and Samuels, each in turn, she saw the first glimmerings of realization in their eyes.

Baila turned to her. "Uhura . . ."

"I know," she said. "I know."

In the meantime Endris went on, his hands sculpting the bright air of the courtyard. He seemed oblivious to the humans, oblivious even to his fellow Rithrim, absorbed as he was in the memory of his people's grief.

"Compelled by their genetic makeup to fight, but unable to vent their aggression on or around Rithra, the warriors decided to leave us. For the first time in our history a caste planned to split off, leaving its sister castes behind. What would they do? Where would they go? We asked these questions.

"The warriors told us there were numerous populations in the galaxy in need of a proficient fighting force—planetary civilizations that would welcome them with open arms. To the other castes, however, the very idea was too shameful to contemplate. The warriors were part of us, and we were part of them; the procreators carried their future generations. How could they hire themselves out to some other race? It would dishonor us all.

"But the warriors would not listen. In fact, they said, they had already agreed to serve an alien government . . . on a planet called Parathu'ul."

"The Parath'aa," repeated Wesley. "Damn!"

Endris looked up at him, suddenly conscious of his surroundings again. "Yes, the Parath'aa. You have heard of them?"

The commodore grunted. "You might say that. And your warriors are working for them?"

"That is our understanding," the governor agreed. "Though we have not heard from our fifth caste since it left Rithra, so we have no way of knowing for certain."

"The mercenaries in the Xaridian systems . . ."

Samuels began. "Captain Kirk called them 'warriors born.'"

The commodore nodded. "A bunch of top-notch fighters, like none we've ever seen before. It makes sense."

"I do not understand," said Endris.

The commodore frowned. "Not too long ago a mysterious fleet began raiding some of our colonies, killing innocent people for no apparent reason. I've got a sneaking suspicion those raiders are your warriors."

The governors looked at one another. Their hands flew in rapid exchanges.

"They're discussing the possibility," Uhura translated without being asked. "And they're conceding that Commodore Wesley could be right."

Finally Endris turned to them again, remorse etched in his face.

"We did not know," he said. "If our sister caste has stooped to murder on behalf of the Parath'aa, our shame is deeper now than ever." He shook his head. "Our dishonor knows no bounds."

"You could redeem yourselves," Wesley suggested. "Our ships have been unable to stop your warriors. Help us—give us some idea of their weaknesses—and we'll be able to put an end to the slaughter."

The governor regarded him. "Do you know what you are asking? If we were to divulge our warriors' weaknesses, and if our revelation led to their blood being shed . . ." He shuddered. "The fifth caste has abandoned us, but we will not betray them."

"We don't want to kill them," Coss interjected. "Just to stop them."

Endris's hands cut the air. "And can you guarantee none of them will perish in the process? Our warriors do not surrender easily, Doctor. If we help you, our betrayal of them will surely lead to their death."

"Sir . . ." said Samuels.

The commodore looked at him. "Yes?"

"We already know one of their weaknesses."

It took Uhura a moment to realize what he was talking about.

Wesley, too, apparently. Then a grim smile took hold of his features. "So we do," the commodore responded. "So we do."

Chapter Thirteen

CHEKOV SIGHED. Finding the raiders was proving a lot tougher than anyone had expected.

Sitting beside him, Sulu raised his gaze from his helm console, turned to the ensign, and said: "Narrow your range by another hundred thousand kilometers."

The Russian complied. "Aye, Mr. Sulu." And then: "Nothing yet."

"Have you tried increasing the portion of the spectrum you are scanning for?"

"Of course."

"Okay, then go to long-range sensors and try heading three-fourteen mark two-four."

A pause. "Still nothing."

"Once again."

Chekov shook his head. Maybe Scotty had been wrong; maybe the negative ions he'd found were a red herring. "Still no sign of them," the ensign commented wearily.

"Don't give up," said Sulu. "Let's move over to section three-fourteen mark one-six."

The ensign nodded. "Aye, scanning now. Nothing."

Chekov swiveled in his seat, looking over at the science console. "Is everything calibrated as we discussed?"

"Aye-aye," said the officer who'd taken Spock's place at the science station.

As for the Vulcan himself, he just sat and watched, the picture of patience and decorum. No doubt he'd have liked to be at the science station himself, but with the captain elsewhere, Spock's place was in the command seat.

Sulu turned back to his monitors and resumed examining the detailed schematics of the sector now under the sensors' gaze. A full array of readings ran across the screen; Chekov could see them from where he sat.

"Pavel, there's a group of free-floating asteroids just at the edge of that sector." He pointed to the quadrant in question. "Try focusing there."

Chekov depressed three buttons, peered into the controls, adjusted the round control on the viewer's side, and then shook his head. "No luck, sir." He sighed. "It's getting pretty hopeless, isn't it?"

"Is that any way for the navigator of the *Enterprise* to talk?" Sulu made a clucking sound. "That's not the attitude that got you through the Maltusian maze back at the Academy."

The Russian looked at him. "You know about that?"

198

Sulu nodded. "News travels—you'd be surprised how far. Even *I* had trouble with the maze."

Chekov smiled a little at the memory. "Ah, well, if you vant me to find your way through the maze, that's one thing. It's all in how you handle the third fork on the fifth level. But this—"

"Is nothing different, just a maze in an unusual configuration," Sulu finished. "Now try mark two-three before we move on." There was a pause and then he added, "The fifth level, you say?"

Chekov chuckled despite himself. Was this the helmsman's way of bolstering his spirits? If so, it was working.

"All right. Let's try heading three-fifteen mark two-six."

"Aye," said Chekov. "Switching sensor to three-fifteen mark two-six. Wait a moment . . . Got it, Sulu!"

"Ensign?" came the Vulcan's voice.

The Russian swiveled in his seat. "I found them, sir. I found the raiders!"

Spock was characteristically calm. "I see." He turned to Palmer at the communications station. "Lieutenant, call the captain to the bridge, please."

Without waiting to be asked, Chekov laid in the required course. "Heading now three-fifteen mark two-six," he announced.

"Increase speed to warp four," said Spock.

"Increasing speed to warp four," Sulu confirmed. As the engines began to whine a little higher, acknowledging the change in speed, the intensity of the bridge crew went up a notch as well.

"Spock to phaser room, go to standby alert, please."

A telltale on Chekov's board switched from amber to green. He nodded to himself.

"Okay, Pavel, exactly where are the raiders?"

"There is a cluster of asteroids in an elliptical orbit just beyond the Gamma Xaridian system. I found over a dozen separate traces leading in that direction."

"Time until arrival?"

"Four hours, seventeen minutes."

"Plenty of time for the captain to map out his plan . . . while we're still on shift." Sulu smiled a wicked grin. "I wouldn't miss this match-up for a month's worth of shore leave."

Chekov returned the smile, if a little grimly, and replied, "Nor vould I."

"Look sharp, people."

The *Enterprise* slowly approached the meteor swarm at the outer edge of the Gamma Xaridian system. Ahead of them floated thousands upon thousands of small chunks of space debris, ranging from several millimeters to several miles in diameter. The swarm itself was miles wide, looking almost endless.

"Mr. Spock?" Kirk didn't even have to complete the question.

"Difficult to be precise, Captain," Spock said. "A number of the asteroids contain highly ionized ore that is interfering with our sensor array. If the raiders are indeed hiding within the asteroid swarm, it will be very difficult to pin them down."

At the moment the *Enterprise* was still a safe distance from the swarm, positioned behind the second moon of Gamma Xaridian XII, the outermost planet in the system. Kirk leaned forward, studying the difficulties that lay before them.

"We don't have any choice," said Kirk. "At least if we're having difficulty detecting them, they'll have a problem detecting us. Deflectors on full. Ahead one-quarter impulse. Take us in, Mr. Sulu."

Sulu took a deep breath. "Ahead one-quarter impulse," and he eased the starship forward.

Slowly the *Enterprise* made its way into the asteroid swarm. Sulu maneuvered the ship around the larger obstacles, but it was impossible for a ship the size of the *Enterprise* to have an entirely smooth trip among objects that size. There was a steady series of thuds as asteroids hit the deflectors and bounced away.

"Where the devil are they?" said Kirk, trying not to let his irritation show.

And then the *Enterprise* shook under the impact of an explosion against one of the starboard shields.

"I believe we've located them, Captain," Spock said.

Once again eight highly maneuverable, highly deadly ships descended upon the *Enterprise*. This time, however, their advantage of maneuverability gave them a remarkable edge; they could hurtle toward the *Enterprise*, fire, and then dart away to hide among the asteroids.

The *Enterprise* phasers blasted out in every direction, but it was impossible to target the ships. The asteroids interfered with every shot as the smaller vessels continued their deadly game of duck-and-run. And every assault, along with the ongoing hammering of the asteroids, was causing further strain on the starship's shields.

"Sulu!" Kirk shouted over the sounds of alarm and the reports of damage from throughout the ship. "Using photon torpedoes, start targeting the meteors themselves. Ignore the raiders and fire on the meteors! If we blast them apart, the additional debris will slow down the raiders!" He did not bother to add, *I hope.*

The helmsman did as he was told, bringing the torpedoes on line, picking some of the larger asteroids, and firing. The torpedoes hurtled from the ship and, carefully aimed at dead center of the targets, blew the asteroids into fragments. Sure enough, the raiders were forced to slow down to contend with yet more space debris—debris that the much larger *Enterprise* could essentially ignore.

The sudden diminishment in the speed of the raiders gave Sulu the slight edge that he needed, and the phasers of the *Enterprise* suddenly started finding their targets. The raiders lurched under the blasts of the weaponry, but again Sulu found himself cursing under his breath. "The raiders' shields are still holding up against our phasers!" he called out.

The same could not be said of the *Enterprise*'s own shields. Blast after blast came in, and when the alarmed call from Scotty came in, Kirk wasn't the least bit surprised.

"Shields buckling!" shouted the chief engineer, as the *Enterprise* bucked once more under blasts from the raiders. "This jury-rigging isn't going to last much longer!"

And at that moment Palmer suddenly spun in her chair and called out, "Captain! Subspace transmission from the *Lexington!*"

"Are they within range? Can they lend assistance?" Kirk demanded.

"No, sir. They're still in orbit around Rithra."

"Put them on, but it better be important and it better be fast!"

The *Enterprise* shook once more. Sparks flew from the engineering station and Ensign Cortez shrieked once and fell backwards.

"Chekov, take over at Engineering!" ordered Kirk. "Palmer, what the hell happened to *Lexington?*"

"This is *Lexington,* Jim," came the surprisingly calm voice of Commodore Wesley. He could, of course, afford to be calm. He wasn't getting shellacked in the middle of a meteor swarm.

Chekov eased Cortez to one side and slid into place at the engineering station. The smell of burning circuitry was thick in his nostrils, and his eyes began to tear as the smoke stung him.

Cortez moaned softly on the floor as Chekov tried to make some sense of the instrumentation that was still functioning. "Shield power barely holding, Captain!" he called out. From the station he could monitor the power rerouting that was taking place, the handiwork of Scotty in Engineering.

He was drawing reserves from all over the ship, shutting down or dampening everything that was nonessential for the purpose of shoring up the phasers and shields. But he was running out of options.

"I hope you've got something useful, Bob!" shouted Kirk. "We're under attack by the raiders, and our phasers aren't punching through their deflectors!"

"They're Rithrim, Jim! A warrior caste—one we didn't know about!"

"Is knowing that going to be of any use to me within the next minute or so?"

"One more hit on shield four will destroy it completely!" Sulu informed him.

Wesley sounded unflappable. "From what we've learned of Rithramen technology, the raiders' shields should be vulnerable to radiation at the higher end of the scale. Try adjusting your phaser frequencies."

Sulu turned to look at Kirk, who gave a quick nod. But Sulu couldn't do it alone. "Chekov! Recalibrate the—"

Chekov turned and shouted, "I heard the commodore, Captain. Already done. Phasers recalibrated."

Kirk nodded in approval. "Sulu! Hold off. If number four shield is that weak, they'll undoubtedly come around and try to make that the main target."

Sure enough, the eight agile ships arced around and approached from the far side, clearly ready to target and blast the number four defense shield into nonexistence. They were not being particularly subtle about it; their growing sense of invulnerability, coupled with the damage to the *Enterprise,* had bolstered their confidence.

"Now, Sulu! Fire!"

Space was illuminated by the play of the phasers against the raiders. On the bridge the offense weaponry sounded different to Kirk—higher-pitched, angrier, as if the *Enterprise* were screaming in fury at such abuse from the upstart smaller ships.

The phasers pierced the shields of the raiders like knives cutting through butter. So powerful was the impact that the lead raider was blasted clean in half, exploding in opposite directions. Raiders on either side of it were hit as well, spiraling to get away and only partly succeeding.

"Sulu! The asteroid at thirty-eight mark nine!" Kirk was indicating a particularly large one that had a flat surface. "Bank shot. Fire!"

Sulu immediately understood the verbal shorthand, did rapid-fire calculations in his head that beat out the computer by half a second, and fired a pinpoint beam.

The unusual composition of the phaser beam caused it to ricochet like a neatly placed pool shot, catching another raider completely off-guard. A raider from another angle saw it coming, but it was a hair too slow, and the starboard engine of the targeted ship was blown clear off. Hopelessly crippled, the raider immediately destroyed itself.

By then Kirk was on his feet. "They're going to try to get away again. But not this time. Sulu, wide-angle phaser blast. There's a hole in the asteroid swarm at twenty mark one-one-four. They'll probably make for that. On my mark, three, two, one, and . . . fire!"

Kirk was dead-on accurate. The wide-angle phaser burst lashed out just as the raiders turned into it. As the Rithramen warriors realized that they'd swung straight into the phaser blast, the *Enterprise* pounded their ships. On such a wide dispersal, the phasers couldn't be as powerful as they normally were. But they didn't need to be, because Kirk's intention was not to destroy but to stun.

In that respect he was completely successful. In the cramped seats of their ships, the marauders were hurled back as the vessels flipped end over end or spiraled out of control. They tried to reach their controls, tried to get away, even tried to blow themselves up. But the phaser blasts cut right through their shielding, and the pounding of the powerful *Enterprise* weapons crushed the consciousness out of their heads.

Four ships now remained in the fleet of mercenaries, floating helpless and silent in front of the starship.

Kirk licked his dried lips once and said, "Mr. Sulu . . . stand down from red alert. Take the raiders' ships in tow. As soon as we're clear of the meteors, I want the occupants of those ships beamed aboard the *Enterprise*. They have a great many questions to answer."

"Jim?" came the voice of Commodore Wesley. "Jim? You still there?"

"Right here, Commodore. It seems"—Kirk studied his nails with an affected air of relaxation—"their shields were vulnerable to phasers set at the high end of the scale. How fortunate that we happened to discover that in time."

There was a pause, and he could almost see the grin at the other end of the comm channel. "That's why you're a legend in your own time, Captain. You always know just what to do."

"True enough, Commodore. Thank you for your kind words. *All* of them."

"Since everything is calm there, we have some business to finish up on Rithra. Can you survive without us for a little while longer?"

"I don't foresee any problems, Commodore."

"Good. *Lexington* out."

McCoy emerged onto the bridge, carrying his medical bag. "You through getting the crap kicked out of us?"

"All done, Doctor."

"Good. Chekov called me to . . . oh, okay. Hold still, Cortez." McCoy knelt next to the injured engineering officer and immediately applied painkiller to Cortez's scorched hands.

Kirk eyed Chekov. "You took it upon yourself to summon Dr. McCoy, Ensign? To inform the ship's doctor, a superior officer, that he should leave sickbay and tend to wounded up here?"

Chekov suddenly felt as if he'd stepped in something. "Mr. Cortez was injured. I thought that—"

"You *thought,* Ensign?"

"Yes, sir."

Kirk hesitated only a moment and then nodded. "Take your position at Navigation, please. You've got a course to set."

Chekov moved immediately to the navigation station. Was he in hot water again?

He didn't think so. On the other hand, the damage he'd already done might have been enough to sour the captain on him for good.

Chapter Fourteen

DAB STOOD IN FRONT OF her procreation center—at least, she thought of it as hers—and looked out at the equipment left there by the humans. The shield generator they had set out to build was only partly finished.

And the humans who'd swarmed over the area a few short hours ago were gone. Nor could she blame them. Taken by a great shadow of mourning, she shook her head.

Now the children would die—slowly, and in pain. And the procreators who were tied to this place by ages-old instinct would eventually die as well, though not before the increasing radiation made them infertile.

It was the most terrible thing Dab could imagine. And to think they had been so close to getting the help they needed. . . .

She heaved a sigh. It was the warriors' fault. If they had not chosen to exercise their instincts on helpless colonists, the Federation people would still be here putting their device together.

No—not the fault of the warriors alone. Because even after the warriors' role in the slaughter had been discovered, the Rithrim might have remained in the humans' favor—had it not been for Endris's refusal to reveal facts that might have aided in the warriors' apprehension.

Nor could Dab herself escape blame. Because if Wesley and his people had asked her for the truth, she could not have said any more than Endris did. It was not something she could have found in her heart, despite the consequences to the procreation center, despite even what the warriors had done. The fifth caste was part of all of them. How could she have helped to hurt them?

And yet she *had* hurt them, hadn't she? The warrior infants would die along with all the others. Her head reeled with thinking about it. The sequence of events was like a circle, a road with no end and no way off. No matter what her choice, or Endris's, Rithrim would have died.

The irony was that the humans had found the information they were looking for; Wesley and the others had realized it was in the palm of their hands. And the warriors would be killed anyway, despite Endris's attempts to protect them.

Dab contemplated the roiling flow of lava beyond the barrier. She imagined she could feel its killing rays as she recalled the meeting in the governors' courtyard.

Wesley had said he did not care what had happened to the fifth caste. He had said he was not on Rithra to judge, that the only thing of importance to him was the fate of the Rithrim at Girin Gatha.

But that was before he learned what the warriors had done to his people. That was before they gave him reason to hate them.

It was not fair. The children had committed no crime. But they would not be spared; no one would be spared. So sad, so sad . . .

Suddenly there was a glimmer of light near the Federation's machines—barely brighter than the ambient light of Girin Gatha, but discernible nonetheless. As Dab watched, the glimmer gave way to five figures.

Federation people, she realized, even before they had become quite solid. Of course—who else would it be? No doubt they'd returned for their equipment. She bit her lip in despair.

And then she realized, amid all the pity she'd been feeling for her own kind, that the humans deserved pity too. After all, hadn't their kin been killed in the warriors' raids? It would have been the height of barbarism not to express her sympathy for their loss.

Gathering herself, she made her way to them over the humpbacked ground. As she approached, they regarded her—with what kind of loathing, she could only imagine.

"Procreator Dab," said one of them—the female human called Uhura. "I'm glad you're here."

Glad? Dab wondered if she'd heard correctly. But Uhura's signs confirmed it. She was indeed glad.

"Why?" Dab asked simply.

"Because I have to leave," Uhura explained. She indicated her companions with a gesture. "We all do."

"I see," replied the procreator, not seeing at all. With her hands she said she understood the leaving but not the gladness.

The human looked at her. "The gladness," Uhura explained, "is because I have a chance to say good-bye. And to wish you luck with the procreation center."

Now Dab was truly confused. "What kind of luck can we have," she asked, "without your shield to keep us safe?"

Uhura smiled. "Did you think we'd leave you here without completing the job we started? Of *course* you'll have our shield—and anything else you need, if it's in our power to give it to you."

The procreator signed her bewilderment. "But the warriors . . ."

"Ah," said the human. "Now I see. You thought we'd hold the warriors' attacks against all of you." She shook her head. "The warriors will be held accountable for what they did. But there's no reason for the rest of you to suffer. All you did was hang on to your beliefs. There's no crime in that."

Dab felt giddy with disbelief. "Then before you depart—"

"Mr. Samuels and his team will make sure the shield projector is operational. In fact, it's almost at that point now; they just had to return to the ship for some parts." Uhura paused. "That *is* what you wanted to hear, isn't it?"

Speechless, Dab used her hands to respond in the affirmative. It was very *much* what she wanted to hear.

"Ready, Lieutenant?" asked Samuels.

Uhura cast a last glance at the tortured vista of Girin Gatha. The place didn't look any different with the Federation's shield in place. Lava still boiled and writhed on the other side of the barrier, and the sea still turned to steam on the far side of the procreation center.

But there was a difference. The radiation that had threatened the procreators and their offspring wouldn't get through anymore. The Rithrim were safe in their little building.

Turning to the procreation center, she saw Dab and a couple of others standing at the front door. She waved; they waved back.

Uhura could still see the gleam in the procreator's eyes when she realized that Commodore Wesley wasn't going to abandon them to their fate after all. She could still feel the warmth of Dab's gratitude.

Uhura nodded. "Yes, Commander. I'm ready."

Samuels flipped open his communicator. "Five to beam up," he said.

It seemed to the communications officer that the transport took a little longer than usual—but then, that was to be expected. While the first officer's engineering crew was to remain on the *Lexington,* she and Samuels were to be relayed down to the Rithrim governors' courtyard.

And indeed, that was where they wound up. Adjusting her visor, Uhura looked around and saw Wesley, Coss, and Baila standing around their regular bench, waiting for her and the first officer to join them. Endris and his fellow governors were there as well, on the other side of the pool.

Somehow, the place looked more cheerful than the last time she'd seen it. Of course, the last time circumstances had been a little different.

As Uhura and Samuels approached the others, the first officer addressed the commodore. "Come here often, sir?"

Baila and the doctor chuckled, but Wesley wasn't laughing.

"It's about time," he told them. "We've been staring at one another for the last five minutes, waiting for our translator to arrive. I was about to break out my holograms of the kids."

"Well," said Uhura, "we're here now. Shall we get started?"

The commodore grunted. "Don't see any reason why not." As Uhura and Samuels joined the others at the bench, he turned to the governors. "Again," he told them, "we are glad for the opportunity to speak with you."

Endris, speaking for the others as usual, waved away the suggestion. "It is we who are glad," he said sincerely.

"That may change when they find out about their warriors," muttered Coss.

Wesley cleared his throat—his way of demanding quiet from the doctor. Nor did Coss miss the cue; he pressed his lips together in a frown.

"No doubt," the commodore began, "you've already communicated with Procreator Dab at Girin

Gatha. And you must know that the facility there has been secured with one of our shield generators."

"It is true," said Endris. "We have spoken with her."

"That generator will be effective for years," Wesley remarked. "You needn't worry about the procreation center for some time to come."

Uhura embellished the statement with expressions of confidence, but they weren't really necessary. The Rithrim trusted that what the commodore had told them was true; she could see it in their eyes.

"We are grateful," Endris said simply. His gestures confirmed it. Then his expression changed. "And what of our fifth caste?" he asked.

"Here it comes," murmured Coss.

Wesley straightened. Without apology he said: "Our ship *Enterprise* encountered your warriors and defeated them in a pitched battle. Some of the ships were destroyed; many more would have been, by the warriors' own hands, if the *Enterprise* hadn't acted quickly. As it is, the surviving warriors will stand trial for their crimes in the Federation courts."

The present-cycle governor showed no anger; Uhura wasn't even sure he was capable of it. Instead, he made a single sign.

Not one of hatred, as they had feared. Not one of resentment. No . . .

It was a sign of relief.

"How *about* that," Uhura whispered.

"What is it, Lieutenant?" asked the commodore.

"They're not angry," replied Baila. "They're *happy* we stopped the warriors."

Wesley turned to his communications officer. "I didn't know you knew sign language, Mr. Baila."

Baila glanced at Uhura and shrugged. "It's amazing what you can do when you put your mind to it."

Apparently, Uhura noted, Mr. Baila had done his homework. She nodded approvingly and then turned her attention back to Endris.

"You seem surprised at our reaction," the governor observed. "Surely you did not think we wished the slaughter of your kind to go on?"

The commodore smiled. "Of course not. We just didn't expect your concern for *our* people to outweigh your concern for your *own.*"

Endris looked puzzled for a moment. "The innocent are the innocent," he explained, "regardless of whether they are Rithrim or human."

Uhura couldn't help but smile at the sentiment. What she really wanted to do was applaud, but that wouldn't have been very appropriate.

The governor looked to Wesley. "Do you still wish to establish an observation post in our space?"

"We do," said the commodore.

"Then it will be arranged. What is more, we would like to have an ongoing dialogue with the Federation. We are considering the possibility of . . . applying for membership in your organization."

Wesley smiled. "We'd be glad to have you," he told the Rithrim. "What kind of dialogue did you have in mind?"

"Perhaps," said Endris, "a small delegation of your people could remain here to facilitate an exchange of information between our race and yours. Also, they could aid in setting up the observation post." He turned to Uhura. "This one has impressed us with her grasp of our language—and with other qualities as well. We would be pleased if she were to lead the delegation."

Uhura realized her mouth was hanging open, and she shut it. "I . . . I don't know what to say," she sputtered.

The commodore turned a benign eye on her. "Say what you feel, Lieutenant."

She shrugged. "I'm honored." For a moment she tried to picture herself here on Rithra for an extended period of time. It would be a great opportunity to learn about the Rithrim and their culture. The chance of a lifetime.

"Honored," she repeated. "However, I must respectfully decline. I hope you understand," she told Endris. "My place is on a starship. That's what I was trained to do; that's what I love."

The present-cycle governor nodded. "I understand very well, Lieutenant. Nor would I wish to take you from your people against your will."

His hands carved signs in the air. Perhaps, they said, the delegation wasn't such a good idea after all. "Perhaps it is wrong to ask someone to live among strangers," Endris said out loud.

"Not at all," Wesley replied. "The Federation has specialists in xenology who are trained to spend long periods of time in cultures other than their own. I'm sure they—"

"Sir?" Baila interjected. He regarded his commanding officer. "If you don't mind, *I* would like to stay on Rithra."

The commodore returned his gaze. "Are you sure about this, Lieutenant?"

Baila nodded. "Pretty sure, sir. You see, when I saw those warrior infants back in the procreation center . . . well, I felt that I was looking at myself, in a way. With the adult warriors gone, those youngsters are going to grow up without role models, without a heritage to draw on. They'll be cut off from something important. And as Uhura will tell you, getting cut off from your heritage is one subject in which I'm an expert." A pause. "I want to be here to see how they handle it . . . and maybe, in some way, to give them a helping hand."

Wesley took a deep breath, let it out. "Lieutenant . . . this wouldn't have anything to do with our differences of late, would it? Because as far as I'm concerned, I'm looking at a new man."

Baila shook his head. "No, sir. My decision has nothing at all to do with that."

The commodore frowned. "Well, in that case"—he turned again to Endris and clapped Baila on the back—"it looks as if we've got someone to head up that delegation, Present-cycle Governor."

Endris nodded. "I am delighted. Welcome, Mr. Baila."

The communications officer inclined his head, then made a rudimentary sign of gratitude with his hands. "Thank you, Present-cycle Governor." He addressed Wesley again. "Commodore, if it's all the same to you, I'd like to get started right now. I haven't got that many friends on the ship anyway and—"

"I understand," Wesley interjected. "We'll send your things down before we break orbit."

Dr. Coss turned to Baila and offered him his hand. "I guess this is good-bye—at least for a while. I'm going to miss you, Lieutenant."

"Same here," said Baila, clasping the proferred hand. "Hell, I'll miss all of you. Even you, Mr. Samuels."

The first officer feigned confusion. "Was that a dig, mister? Don't forget, you're still under my command until I say so—and the comm board's long overdue for a full diagnostic check." He smiled. "Then again, what isn't? Have a hell of a good time, Lieutenant."

"I will," Baila assured him.

Finally the communications officer turned to Uhura. "What can I say?" he asked her.

"Say you'll keep in touch, *amuntu*."

He nodded. "I'll do that, Uhura. You can bet your ancestors' teeth on it." Taking her hand in his, he squeezed it. His grip was as warm as a jungle breeze.

"Come on," said Wesley. "Let's get out of here before I break down and cry. I don't think that's the kind of image we want to present to our new allies."

Reluctantly Baila released Uhura's hand and took a step back. But she knew it would be a long time before she forgot the look in those dark, dark eyes of his.

The commodore turned to Endris and his fellow governors. "We'll be going now. But you'll be hearing from the Federation again before long. And of course, in the meantime you'll have Mr. Baila to keep you company."

Endris was silent, but his gestures bade them luck on their journey. "Perhaps we will meet again," he said.

"You never know, Present-cycle Governor. Good luck to you and to your people." Wesley took out his communicator and addressed his transporter chief. "Four to beam up, Lieutenant."

"Four, sir?"

"That's right," the commodore confirmed. "Mr. Baila is staying here with the Rithrim for the time being."

There was a pause, and then: "I understand, sir."

Uhura cast a last glance at Baila. He winked at her, as if to say, I'll be fine here, really I will.

A moment later the transporter beam reeled them in, and she was standing with Wesley, Samuels, and Coss on the platform. The doctor removed his visor as if he couldn't wait to get the darn thing off.

"Remind me," he said, "to send some of these down to Baila. He's going to need a bunch of them."

"That he is," agreed the commodore.

"You know," Samuels remarked, "I hope everything works out down there."

"For Baila?" Uhura responded. "I'm sure it will."

The first officer shook his head. "Not for Baila. I'm talking about the shield generator." Reaching into his shoulder pouch, he pulled out a machine component and shrugged. "Somehow we had this piece left over. None of us could figure out where it went."

"Damn it, Samuels," said Wesley, his eyes darkening, "we can't leave orbit until that generator is—"

"I'm kidding, I'm kidding," the first officer assured him, holding up his hands. "It was just a *joke,* sir."

Suddenly the commodore grinned. "I knew that.

Do you think after we've served together for as long as we have that there's a trick in your bag I *don't* know?"

And they all had a good laugh—even Samuels. In fact, Uhura noted, it was the first officer who laughed the loudest.

Chapter Fifteen

As Kirk rode the turbolift up to the bridge, he thought about the Rithramen warriors' code of honor. As distraught as they were over having been captured rather than killed, they had no compunction whatsoever about revealing the identity of their employers— or, for that matter, about providing the captain with a complete list of the components they'd obtained.

However, they claimed to have no idea what the equipment was for. Kirk hoped his officers had made some headway on that count by themselves.

The doors opened and he stepped out onto the bridge. A moment later Sulu turned in his seat to greet him.

"Did your visit pay off, sir?"

"In spades, Mr. Sulu, in spades." Turning to Chekov, he said: "Ensign, lay in a course back to Parathu'ul."

"Course plotted and laid in, sir."

"Mr. Sulu, engage at warp six."

"Warp six. Aye, sir."

"Very good, gentlemen." Moving to join Spock, the captain overheard Chekov mutter, "I feel like a soccer ball, the way we're bouncing around this quadrant."

He also heard Sulu's reply: "But, Chekov, how else does one become a good navigator? Practice, practice, and more practice."

There was an anguished sigh from Chekov.

"Fifth level indeed," Sulu muttered under his breath.

Rounding the deck, Kirk stopped at Spock's side. The science officer was deeply immersed in his study of the information downloaded from the raiders' vessels.

Noting the captain's presence, Spock straightened and turned off the hooded viewer. "It is worse than I expected," he said.

Kirk looked at him. "What do you mean?"

The Vulcan frowned. "The Parath'aa now have the technological components to build a rather formidable weapon."

"Aye, that they do," Scott added as he walked over from the engineering station. "Mr. Spock, your hypothesis checks out with the technical profiles I've got in me office."

"Elaborate, gentlemen," Kirk prompted.

The Vulcan complied. "The Parath'aa appear to possess the wherewithal to build a plasma cannon," Spock explained.

The captain whistled. "I remember reading classified reports on that program. Whatever happened to it?"

Spock shrugged. "Scientists at Starfleet Command developed the technology up to the point of manufacture. They even constructed a small-scale, working model. Its range was quite limited, but it did cause a great deal of damage. A full-scale version could level a world."

Kirk shook his head. "Wonderful."

Scotty nodded. "Aye, sir, it's a treacherous beastie. The plasma it uses is essentially ionized gas, with electrons and positive ions combined in such a way as t' neutralize the electrical charge and allow it t' be controlled through magnetic fields. When the plasma comes into contact with a force shield, the conflict of energies can be devastating."

He harrumphed. "The weapons experts at Starfleet could never find a good reason to include that kind of weaponry aboard a starship. Not only that, the damned thing would tax the warp engines beyond safety limits. Personally I'm happy they never built the full-scale model."

"But now the Parath'aa, under a belligerent government, possess the ability to build just such a cannon," Kirk stated.

"But why would they want a cannon if they already rule their world?" Scott asked.

"Why indeed?" echoed Spock.

Kirk wrestled with the question in his own mind—and came up with a grim possibility.

"Mr. Spock, which populated worlds are closest to Parathu'ul?"

"You dinna think . . ." began Scotty.

The captain regarded him. "We can't rule it out, Mr. Scott. Spock?"

"The Xaridian colonies, sir."

"And the next closest?"

The Vulcan paused to process the information in his mind. It never ceased to amaze Kirk that Vulcans could process and retain huge amounts of raw information. On the other hand, to discipline their minds, they gave up their capacity for emotion—something the captain was sure he would never want to do.

"The next nearest populated system," Spock began, "would be outside Federation boundaries—perhaps within the Gorn Hegemony. Of course the Parath'aa are also within reach of unexplored territory."

"Do you suspect they would use the cannon to go after the Gorn?" Kirk wondered out loud.

"Doubtful, Captain."

"Captain Kirk," Sulu called from the helm. "I've picked up movement away from Parathu'ul. A number of blips on our long-range sensors."

"Course?" Kirk began swiftly moving back to his command chair.

"At present heading," replied Chekov, "they are going directly into unrestricted space. Ships moving at warp five."

Kirk turned around to watch Spock process the information from his station. "Are they the marauders, Spock?"

"Negative," the Vulcan replied. "The configuration is typical of the Parath'aa. They are using their standard pentagon flight formation—but our sensors detect something in the center of the formation as well. Something held there by a tractor beam."

"My God," Kirk said quietly. "The cannon!"

"Most likely, sir," confirmed Spock. "And they have extended their shields to protect it."

Chekov turned to Kirk and added, "Sir, the wessels are moving toward the Cygni Maxima system. They will arrive in four hours, fifteen minutes."

Before Kirk could even ask, he noted that the Vulcan had already begun calling up charts on Cygni Maxima. He smiled grimly and waited a few moments for Spock to issue his report.

As expected, the science officer turned and said, "Cygni Maxima is a yellow star with seven planets and two asteroid belts. The *Hood* charted it some seventeen years ago; their report indicated sentient life on the system's fourth planet. At the time, the inhabitants were rated several points below our own society and their planet has been declared off-limits to all Federation space traffic."

"Why would the Parath'aa want to go all the way to Cygni Maxima, then?" Sulu wondered aloud.

Kirk replied without looking at him. "Conquest, Mr. Sulu. Those pompous government leaders on Parathu'ul have already subjugated their own people —and now they have the means to subjugate *other* worlds."

"A logical premise, Captain," Spock noted dryly from his post.

Kirk was left with a hard choice. He could either confront the government on Parathu'ul with his suspicions or he could have the *Enterprise* pursue the convoy. If he was right about the Para'thaa's intentions, the convoy would use the cannon to destroy a helpless race.

But what if there were other cannons under construction—maybe on the verge of being launched? And there was another, more practical question: could the *Enterprise* stop a weapon that was powerful enough to tear through her shields?

There was no time to debate, so he chose to go with his gut.

"Chekov, plot an intercept course. Sulu, engage at warp six-point-five. Have Engineering make sure the engines are in top shape. Palmer, go to red alert."

"Aye, sir," came the crisp reply.

As Kirk took his center seat, the sirens rang out and the lights flashed red. The captain leaned back in his chair and allowed himself a moment for introspection.

Once again, after a relatively short time, he was asking his crew to go into battle. Sure, they'd succeeded against the Rithramen mercenaries, but now they were up against a different kind of threat, a weapon of amazing power. Kirk needed to think strategically, to plan his actions in advance, so that little would be left to chance.

"Lieutenant Palmer, let me have intraship, please," he called out. A beep acknowledged that the communications system was activated. Thumbing a button on his armrest, he said: "This is the captain. We are about to enter politically unaligned space, where we may have to engage a pack of Parath'aat ships. Please prepare for combat."

Kirk paused. "I know this is the fourth time I've asked this of you in the last couple of days. I wish the circumstances were otherwise, but I see no choice. All I can ask is that you give me your best effort. Captain out."

Spock walked down to Kirk and offered, "We have four hours. Do you require sustenance?"

"No, Spock. I require this to be over. The Parath'aa are proving to be quite an annoying race."

Spock nodded. "They have yet to gain the wisdom to unite their planet with a singular vision."

"All this fighting . . ." Kirk said wearily. "It's so pointless. Sometimes I'm a diplomat, sometimes I'm an explorer—and now I'm forced to be a soldier. And I don't think there's much reason behind this insanity."

"I understand, sir. You do not seek the battles; you seek only understanding. It is . . . most commendable."

The captain looked up at him with a small smile. "Why, thank you, Spock."

The two friends returned their attentions to the bridge crew's pre-encounter preparations. Lieutenant Commander Giotto reported to the bridge a few minutes later, carrying a tricorder.

"Captain," he said, "I've studied Starfleet intelligence reports on the Parath'aa. Their ships are conventional warp-capable vessels. They tend to be smaller than our starships and therefore have smaller crews. And they prefer to design their ships for specific functions." A pause. "Apparently the ships we picked up on sensor scan match the configuration recorded for defense."

"But now they're using them for offense," Kirk noted. "Go on."

Giotto frowned. "They use standard phaser arrays and photon torpedoes. I don't see any reason why we can't outrun or outgun them if it comes to that."

Kirk nodded. "Thank you, Mr. Giotto." He turned to his helmsman. "Mr. Sulu, work with the phaser room. Run simulations on such attack patterns and see how good we are at targeting their engines and weapons. I'll take nothing less than one hundred percent accuracy."

"Aye, sir," Sulu said. He toggled his communicator for a direct link with the phaser room.

"Martine here," came the response.

The captain was pleased to see that Martine was on duty. He always felt safer with her commanding the phaser crew. She was quick-witted and thoroughly efficient.

"Specialist Martine," said Sulu, "this is the bridge. I'm sending down information on our potential opponents, and we're going to run simulations. We have about four hours before contact—plenty of time to get ourselves ready. Agreed?"

"Agreed, Mr. Sulu. We're receiving the information now. It looks as if we can run our routine patterns first, modifying as we go along."

As always, Kirk noted, Martine was ready to start with the rule book and then throw it out when things got imaginative. Her skill had certainly helped make a difference against the Rithramen ships.

During the next few hours, Sulu and Martine ran simulations. The first battle had a computed accuracy rate of 67 percent. Far too low for either one to be happy. They had improved to an 89 percent rate before both agreed they needed a break.

Meanwhile, as Kirk observed, the other officers were busy with their own preparations. Chekov was reviewing the star charts for this sector of space. He and Spock compared notes on space phenomena that previous probes had somehow missed. With time on his hands, the Vulcan had his science officers make observations of the nebula, adding the information to the massive library computer.

Yeoman Martha Landon came up to the bridge with a tray of cups, which she took to the duty personnel. As usual, Spock eschewed any drink, but the others thanked her for her thoughtfulness. Landon lingered a moment by the navigation console, where Chekov was painfully intent on his readouts.

"How are you holding up, Ensign?" she asked.

Chekov looked up, a bit startled by the question. "Oh, ah, yes, yeoman . . . ?"

"Martha Landon," she replied with a smile.

"Thank you," he replied, apparently noticing her tightly wound blond hair and bright eyes for the first time.

Smiling again, this time with even more enthusiasm, Landon spun on her heel and moved briskly off the bridge.

Kirk watched the interplay and suppressed a smile. This probably wasn't the best time to build relationships, but it was hard to suppress human nature.

He updated his log and had Palmer send it out to both Starfleet and the *Lexington*. This way Wesley would be as well informed as possible when they met again near Parathu'ul.

"Captain, sensors have placed us within twenty minutes of contact with the Parath'aat formation," Spock announced.

Kirk nodded. "Palmer, open a channel." He paused, listening for the familiar beep-beep announcing that the signal was open. "This is Captain Kirk of the *Enterprise*. We know what you're aiming to do, and we can't allow it. We trust that you'll be willing to return the stolen Federation equipment. Please reply."

It took a few moments, but a response came in—on audio signal only. The captain immediately recognized the speech patterns of the Parath'aa.

"We are hearing you Kirk, but we are *not* complying. I am claiming this solar system in the name of the Parath'aa, and I am advising you to be backing off. We are, after all, being prepared to deal with hostile intervention."

Those words caught Kirk by surprise, but he recovered quickly. Leaning forward in his command chair, he snapped, "The people of Cygni Maxima are in no position to defend themselves; we will not stand by while you attack them. This ship is ready to stop you any way we can. You have been warned."

"Once again, Captain Kirk, *we* are warning *you*. You may have been denying us admission to your precious interplanetary clique, but you won't be denying us *this* system. We are having the means to be doing as we please. Now it will please us to destroy your ship."

The signal ended; Palmer shrugged at Kirk. No further communication was likely.

"Red alert," the captain ordered. "Sulu, have phasers on line at full power. Let's see what you and Martine have come up with. Shields at maximum." Hitting his communications button, Kirk said, "Bridge to Engineering. Scotty, are we ready for battle?"

"If ye have to fight, she's ready, sir," Scott replied. "But I canna guess what'll happen when they fire the plasma cannon. I've got damage control teams on standby, starting with life support and weaponry."

"Very good, Scotty. Sulu, bring us within phaser range, but be ready to maneuver. Mr. Chekov, be ready for some quick calculations. Ultimately I want to position us between the fleet and the planet."

Both Sulu and Chekov replied in the affirmative and set about their work. The lights dimmed to a red glow, and the bridge emptied of nonessential personnel. Spock hunched over his viewer while Kirk leaned over Sulu's shoulder to watch the sensors.

"Captain," said the Vulcan, "I'm reading a power buildup from the plasma cannon. If they constructed it according to specifications, it will take forty-five seconds to build to an initial charge. After a discharge, it will recycle in ten-second intervals."

Kirk turned to the helm. "That's your window of opportunity, Sulu. We'll have that much time to attack between blasts."

"Target the cannon, sir?" asked the helmsman.

Kirk shook his head. "No, Lieutenant," he said grimly. "Target the Parath'aa vessels." He grunted.

"The question will be whether we can knock out enough of their ships to loosen their hold on the cannon—*before* they knock *us* out."

"Aye, sir," Sulu acknowledged. "It'll be tight." His voice always slipped into a deeper register when the pressure was on.

The *Enterprise* moved within range, and the five Parath'aat ships did not slow down. On the viewscreen, the crew could see the plasma cannon. It was large and bulky, about half the size of one of the ships. Two boxlike shapes were attached to either side of the mammoth barrel; the whole thing was laced with wiring and support equipment.

Not very elegant, Kirk mused. But then, it had been built by the Parath'aa to be a weapon and not an object of beauty.

His musings stopped when he saw that the cannon—trapped in the center of the convoy by five bright tractor beams—was beginning to glow at one end. It was a dangerous, fiery red glow. The crew watched the glowing end revolve slowly, moving away from the planet and toward the *Enterprise*. With every passing second, the glow increased in intensity until it seemed like a volcano ready to erupt.

"Hold on!" Kirk cried out. A moment later the starship's shields crackled with the impact of the plasma burst. Such was the power of the plasma that while it sprayed the shields for only a fraction of a second, the ship shook for what seemed like an eternity.

The bridge personnel were buffeted in their seats, and the red alert lighting blinked off for a moment.

When the ship regained its equilibrium, Kirk demanded a status report.

"Shields held but are down to seventy-three percent efficiency," Chekov announced.

"Sulu, fire phasers!" Kirk ordered.

Twin beams of crimson energy lashed out from the starship and scored two direct hits on the shields of the lead Parath'aat vessel.

"Three of their screens are down," Spock observed, without straightening from his post.

"Fire again," Kirk snapped.

The ship's phasers slashed through space and made direct contact with the Parath'aat ship. At the same time, two of the Parath'aat ships fired their own phasers. As the *Enterprise*'s shields absorbed the attack, the crew felt the impact, but it was minor compared to that of the plasma cannon.

Sulu announced, "Lead ship has lost engine power. Plasma cannon will ignite in five seconds."

"Sulu, hard to starboard," Kirk called.

"Aye, sir," came the response—just as the cannon erupted once more. With the ship in motion, the plasma hit only a portion of the shields, but it was more than enough to overload a number of ship's systems. The background speakers spit out a steady stream of status reports and calls for damage crews.

"We have lost the number six shield. Other shields being deployed to compensate," Spock reported. He turned to the captain. "Sir, the plasma is eating away at shield integrity. The two forms of energy are most volatile in combination. We will not last long if we sustain many more direct hits."

"Fire!" Kirk called out.

Sulu stabbed at the controls; the phaser beams lanced through the shields of a Parath'aat ship, hitting the hull. Then, swiveling the targeting controls, he brought the phasers to bear on another vessel, one directly before the *Enterprise*. After firing again, he watched with satisfaction as the phasers hit pay dirt a second time.

"We've knocked three ships out of combat," Sulu announced with a sly smile. "Plasma cannon rebuilding its charge. One ship firing photon torpedo."

Kirk gripped the arms of his chair and ordered the ship to come about at increased speed. The maneuver was successful; the torpedo missed by a good measure.

However, the two remaining Parath'aat ships managed to turn about and aim the cannon in the starship's direction. The plasma beam lanced out and smacked right into the starship.

Leslie was jarred loose from his position near the engineering console; Chekov nearly lost his seat as well. Sulu rode out the impact by grabbing the sides of the helm and then righting himself. Again, lights flickered, and the increased background noise told Kirk the damage-control teams were going to be busy.

He looked about the bridge quickly and then studied the viewscreen. The cannon crackled silently in space, like a snake ready to lash out with its forked tongue.

Sulu looked at his board and said, "Cannon will be ready in eight seconds."

"Another hit will cause structural damage," Spock noted calmly.

"Sulu, z plus five thousand meters, now!" Kirk called out.

Once again the maneuver was successful, and the cannon fire missed them, but with less room to spare than Kirk would have liked.

"Let's finish this," the captain said. "Sulu, fire phaser barrage and photon torpedo spread at the remaining ships. Overload their shields—I want a good shot at the cannon."

Sulu acknowledged the order and then spoke into his communicator grid, "Okay, Martine, let 'er rip as we practiced!"

Kirk watched the forward viewscreen with interest as the image brightened with the light show. It became apparent that their attack was overtaxing some of the enemy ships' systems—but not so much as he'd hoped.

Sulu turned in his seat long enough to tell Kirk, "Both ships still have tractor locks on the cannon, sir. It'll fire any second."

"Scott to captain. We're losin' system controls left and right. Some o' the power couplings are fused. Another plasma hit and we're sure to go off line with the warp engines."

Gritting his teeth and ignoring the warning, Kirk barked: "Fire again, Sulu! Give 'er everything you've got!"

Coolly, Sulu nodded, turned, and hit the firing controls. All officers watched as phasers and photon torpedoes twinkled in space en route to their target.

Seconds before they got there, the cannon fired again. The resulting explosion nearly whited out the viewer and sent shock waves with enough force to shake the crew up again.

Kirk hung on to his armrests for dear life. "Spock," he called, "status!"

The Vulcan took a quick glance at a screen above his station. "The cannon is no longer under Parath'aat tractor control. However, they must have some remote link with the firing mechanism; energy in the cannon is building up for another discharge in"—he consulted his monitor—"seven seconds."

Scotty's voice was frantic as it came in over the intercom. "Engineering to Captain Kirk! The hull's been breached, sir! We're sealin' off decks six and seven." And then: "Captain, we canna take any more o' this!"

Kirk stared at the clearing viewscreen, with its perspective on the turning cannon. *That's all right, Mr. Scott,* he thought. *With any luck, we won't have to.*

"Lock phasers on to the cannon," he said out loud. "Prepare photon torpedoes."

"Phasers locked," Sulu announced coolly. "Photon torpedoes ready."

"Brace yourselves, everyone. Fire!"

On the screen the cannon sparkled with each hit of phaser or photon torpedo. For a moment nothing happened.

Then, with a massive burst of lethal energies, it vanished.

Kirk knew what would come next. "Mr. Sulu, heading two-one-three mark fifty-four!"

Sulu's hands skittered over his board like frantic

insects, but the *Enterprise* wasn't operating at peak efficiency. The ship felt sluggish as it moved to avoid the imminent shock wave.

Before it hit, the captain had time to think: Wouldn't that be ironic? To kill the thing and then get caught in its death throes!

But even hobbled as it was, the *Enterprise* proved fast enough. The shock wave hit the ship almost as hard as the cannon impact, but it didn't shake the *Enterprise* apart.

Kirk breathed a sigh of relief as Spock rose and peered into his viewer. "The cannon is destroyed, Captain. Shields restored, but still at only minimal efficiency."

The captain nodded. "Palmer, open a channel to the Parath'aat flagship."

"Hailing frequencies open, Captain."

"Enterprise to the Parath'aat commander."

This time the response was visual as well as audible. "This is Commander Chak," said the typically Parath'aat visage on the screen. Chak was sweating profusely, and he had a deep cut over one eye, from which blood was flowing freely.

"Chak, we have shown that we mean business. Cygni Maxima is off limits to the Parath'aa. Your people are guilty of murder, wanton destruction, and outright theft."

A smile crossed Chak's face "I am being a warrior, Kirk. I am knowing no life other than conquest. It has been taking our faction years to be gaining control of our world. I will not be going meekly."

Kirk nervously looked at Spock to see if Chak was

initiating any sort of self-destruct mechanism, such as those used by the Rithrim. Spock checked his equipment and silently shook his head, indicating that suicide was not a possibility.

The captain returned his gaze to the screen. "Tell me, Chak, what did your people hope to accomplish?"

"What you were denying us, Kirk. Our people were being united under one rule; we were being ready to deal with the other worlds in space. We were wanting to be a part of your all-so-mighty Federation, but you were saying we were too barbaric, that we were showing no respect for 'the rights of the individual.' Pah. Someone was fearing us, Kirk, and was seeing to it we could not be belonging.

"But we were being between the Gorn and the Federation, and in too strategic a position to be being left alone for long. We were deciding we would not wait for someone else to be taking us over and controlling our destiny. So we were making plans. We were using some of our wealth to hire Federation scientists and using them to learn everything your ambassadors would never be sharing with us. So many skeletons in your closet, Kirk. Tsk-tsk."

Chak seemed to be enjoying himself despite his wounds, but behind him Kirk could see repair crews putting out fires and a medic tending to an injured crewman. The Parath'aat ship seemed to have sustained far more damage than the *Enterprise*.

"Your scientists," Chak went on, "were telling

us about the one weapon you did not possess: the plasma cannon. They were telling us how to find the equipment we needed. So all it took was to be finding a manner in which to be acquiring the necessary components. Fortunately we were having an earlier contact with the Rithrim and were knowing their services were available. It was being mutually beneficial. Everything was going along quite smoothly."

Chak's expression changed to one of restrained bitterness. "Excepting for you. We did not be counting on the Federation to be finding us out so quickly. We were finding it necessary to be accelerating our schedule and to be deciding to leave orbit with just one operational cannon. There are being others, of course, under construction. We are not being easy to stop, Kirk."

The captain looked grim and angry when he chose to respond. "On the contrary, Chak. We're putting you out of business. Today. Our sensors show that all five of your ships are crippled and wouldn't make it through another battle. And as for those other cannons under construction—Starfleet will be by to dismantle them and recover the parts. In short, you're through."

Kirk walked in front of the helm, moving closer to the viewscreen for dramatic impact. "Now you can play your bluff to the hilt, or we can talk about beaming your survivors aboard for transport back to Parathu'ul. The choice is yours."

The screen went blank just as surprise registered on Chak's face. Kirk nodded, having gotten some satisfaction out of the confrontation. Then he looked around his bridge. "Stand down to yellow alert, Mr. Spock. What's our status?"

"We have sustained damage on four decks and had one serious hull breach. Repair teams are already working on the breach. Mr. Scott reports that we retain limited warp capability."

"Not too bad, Mr. Spock," Kirk said. He hit a button on his armrest and called down to sickbay.

"McCoy here, Jim."

"How bad was it?"

"We lost a man in Engineering when systems shorted out—a freak accident—and five more when the hull was breached." A pause. "My God, Jim, did you have to make that battle last so long?"

Kirk grimaced at the toll. All this for a few power-hungry despots. "I wish it were otherwise, Bones. I'll be down soon. Kirk out." He put his hand on the bridge of his nose and squeezed. The tension and adrenaline that had kept him going were gone now. He took a deep breath and stood up.

"Mr. Chekov, plot us a course back to Parathu'ul. Sulu, Palmer, please coordinate with Chak's people and see if they require any assistance. If not, we'll follow them back. Let's get to it."

Next he turned to Spock. "You have the conn," he told the Vulcan.

Spock nodded and moved to the command position even as Kirk was abdicating it.

Satisfied that things were finally coming to a conclusion, the captain stepped onto the upper deck and surveyed his crew. A faint smile crossed his face, and he paused before entering the turbolift.

"You all performed quite well," he said. Faces turned toward him. "Mr. Sulu, my compliments to Specialist Martine and the phaser crew. Enjoy your rest—it's well earned."

Then he entered the lift and went back to his quarters, desperate for just a few hours' rest.

Chapter Sixteen

UHURA WAS PACKING UP her things when she heard the beep. Turning, she said, "Come on in."

She had a feeling who it would be. When the door slid aside, it only confirmed her hunch. Commodore Wesley smiled as he entered.

"Getting set to go?" he asked rhetorically, noting the half-full duffel and the odds and ends spread out on the bed.

Uhura nodded. "I didn't want to leave the packing for the last minute. It wouldn't do to keep two starships waiting while I try to find my toothbrush."

The commodore chuckled. "No. It wouldn't." A pause. "Uhura, it's been a long time since I proposed something important to a beautiful young woman. But . . . well, I've lost Baila—just when I was starting to value his services again, too. And that leaves me one communications officer short."

She smiled. "Are you asking me to stay on?"

"I am."

Uhura folded her arms over her chest. "You must know what my answer's going to be."

Wesley regarded her. "Lieutenant, if there's one thing that's constant in this galaxy, it's uncertainty. I don't take *anything* for granted." And then, in a more congenial voice: "I'm in a position to offer incentives, Uhura. Opportunities. A lieutenant commandership wouldn't be out of the question."

She sighed. "I'm almost tempted to let you go on. I can see how you get people like Samuels and Dr. Coss; it's hard to say no when someone makes you feel this wanted."

He looked rueful. Jilted, she thought. "But . . ."

"But my heart's on the *Enterprise.* Where she goes, I go." She shrugged. "I guess that sounds pretty corny, doesn't it?"

The commodore shook his head. "No. Not at all. That kind of loyalty is one of the qualities I admire in you. I hope Jim Kirk knows how damned lucky he is to have you on his bridge."

"Well," Uhura said, "between you and me, it wouldn't hurt if you were to ask after me now and then. Just to, you know, *remind* him."

Wesley laughed. "I'll do that little thing," he assured her. And then, as an afterthought: "If you change your mind, Lieutenant, let me know."

"If I change my mind," she said, "I will."

Kirk sat back in his seat and contemplated the vast sweep of Parathu'ul on the main viewscreen. The *Potemkin* was visible as a gleaming pindot on the horizon. The starship had arrived only hours after the

Enterprise, making it obvious to Silva and his people that the Federation meant business.

Tapping the appropriate stud on his armrest, the *Enterprise*'s commanding officer cleared his throat. After all, they'd be listening to this back at Starfleet Command.

"Captain's log, stardate 3034.6. We have escorted what was left of the Parath'aat vessels back to their homeworld. What's more, with the help of Captain Callas and the *Potemkin,* we've persuaded the Parath'aat leaders to give up their dreams of conquest and to relinquish the Federation equipment they were using to make additional plasma cannons. Nor will they be able to hold back any of their ill-gotten gains, thanks to Mr. Spock's comprehensive list of missing machinery and components."

Kirk paused. "As for the Federation scientists who helped them . . . we have no extradition treaty with the Parath'aa. However, with nothing left for them to do on Parathu'ul, I don't expect they'll be welcome there much longer. And when they leave, we'll be there to take them into custody. We'd better be—unless we want them rubbing elbows with the Romulans.

"As for the Rithramen raiders—or more accurately, the *survivors* among the raiders—I can't find it in my heart to forgive them, not after all the bloodshed they caused. But I think I'm beginning to understand them. I see them staring out at me from their incarceration, and they look lost—just as lost as I might be if I were separated from the things that make me what I am. It's unfortunate that their calling is such a bloody one—unfortunate for all of us.

"In any case, the *Lexington* will be here any moment to accept the Rithrim and take them to Starbase Eighty-three, where they'll stand trial for their crimes. At that point, I expect, I'll also have my communications officer returned to me."

The captain scowled, inwardly adding *I hope*. There was no underestimating Wesley's powers of persuasion. If he'd had to bet, Kirk would have bet that Uhura would come back to the *Enterprise*. But that was by no means a sure thing.

"End of log entry."

"Captain Kirk?"

He turned at the sound of his name. "Yes, Palmer?"

"I have the *Lexington*, sir. Commodore Wesley."

"Put him through," the captain told her.

A moment later Bob Wesley's image filled the viewscreen. "Good to see you again, Jim. I trust your prisoners are ready for transport?"

"Good to see you too, Commodore. And yes— they're as ready as they'll ever be."

Kirk could see Uhura behind Wesley, at the communications post. She looked pretty comfortable there. Had she fallen for the commodore's wiles after all?

Only one way to find out. And why drag out the suspense? "Do you mind if I retrieve my communications officer before I start beaming over the Rithrim? That way she won't get lost in the shuffle—a possibility you're no doubt counting on."

Uhura stood, and the look on her face made Kirk's heart sink. "Captain, if it's all right with you, I'd like to stay on the *Lexington*—"

Damn, Kirk thought. I should never have let Wesley

get his hooks into her. I should never have let her out of my sight.

"—for a few hours," Uhura finished. "Just long enough to see the Rithrim and give them an idea of what's ahead for them."

Kirk tried to conceal his surprise. "For . . . a few hours?" He shrugged. "Of course, Lieutenant. Whatever you feel you need."

But his first reaction hadn't escaped the commodore. "For a second there, Jim, you thought she was leaving the *Enterprise,* didn't you? Come on, admit it."

The captain didn't flinch. "Not even for a fraction of a second," he replied. "Even though I knew you'd give her your best shot, and then some."

Wesley smiled. "Treat her right, Jim, or I'll be back for her."

"I always have treated her right," Kirk assured him, glancing at Uhura, "and I always will."

Uhura grinned. Fortunately she was the modest type; otherwise, he'd have been afraid this would go to her head.

"You know," said the commodore, "I started this mission with two senior communications officers, and now I've got none. Where's the justice in that?" He shook his head. "Speak with you later, Jim."

The captain nodded. "Later," he agreed. And then, before Palmer could break off the link: "Welcome back, Lieutenant."

The communications officer returned his gaze. "It's nice to *be* back, sir."

Chapter Seventeen

THE FINAL SPARKLES disappeared and Lieutenant Uhura stood on the transporter platform. She beamed happily at Transporter Chief Kyle, who flashed her a smile in return. His reassuring demeanor always gave her an immediate feeling of safety when she returned to the *Enterprise*.

"Glad to have you back, Lieutenant," Kyle said.

"Trust me, Chief, I'm the one who's glad. See you on the rec dec later?"

"Wouldn't miss it," he replied. With that covered, she hefted her bag and strolled out of the transporter room, determined to get right back into the swing of shipboard life. What she really missed, she decided, was her own bed. Nice as the guest quarters were aboard the *Lexington,* she mused, nothing could replace her very own bed. She'd learned that as a little girl back in Koyo.

On her way to the officers' quarters, she exchanged frequent greetings with crewmen. It dawned on her just how many of the crew she knew face-to-face, despite the fact that she spent most of her duty time on the bridge. Sure, she could recognize just about everyone's voice on the comm channels, but faces, personalities, individual traits—she knew so many of them. And most were her friends, something people really needed on extended deep-space duty.

As soon as she entered her cabin, she realized she wasn't all that tired and decided to grab a drink in the mess hall, hoping to run into her colleagues. It was either that or sit in front of the desktop computer, running the last few days' worth of bulletin board messages. No contest—she definitely needed the human touch. With a smile she spun on her heel and headed right back into the corridor.

Chekov and Palmer were finishing a meal when Uhura entered the large mess room. Shifts were about to change, and people were coming and going at a rapid pace. Most stopped, though, to welcome Uhura back in their midst. She went right to her fellow bridge officers and exchanged brief hugs with them. Palmer gestured for Uhura to sit while Chekov went to get her a cup of coffee.

"So, how'd things go, Palmer?" Uhura inquired.

"You heard about the fireworks, so you know it was certainly no milk run," the other woman replied.

"And how did our young navigator do?"

Palmer glanced at Chekov, who was just removing the cup from the food dispenser. Turning her attention back to Uhura, she answered, "He had his rough times, but he came through when things got tight. Oh, and I think there might be something developing between him and Yeoman Landon. At least she seems interested. He's barely noticed."

She grinned as Uhura's eyes widened a bit at the gossip. Palmer paused, looked thoughtful, and added, "Still, he seems preoccupied. You know, concerned about his performance."

As Chekov returned to the table, Palmer smiled at him. The ensign returned the friendly gesture and set the coffee in front of Uhura.

"Hmmm," she said. "Cinnamon. Nice touch, Pavel. Thanks. How were things for you?"

"Not as bad as they might have been. I'm still in Starfleet, aren't I?"

Uhura chuckled and asked, "It wasn't that bad, was it?"

Chekov suppressed a grimace and then replied, "It felt like it, Lieutenant."

"And what's this I hear about you and Yeoman Landon?"

Chekov snapped his head up in astonishment. "What are you talking about?"

Uhura smiled and played with him. "We hear these things, even on other starships, Ensign."

The Russian cleared his throat, too embarrassed for words. "Ah, yes, of course." He stood a bit too quickly, hoping no one saw the red creep up from his collar. "I'll let you two talk. Yes, that's right, er, talk. Me, I'm going to escape before Meester Sulu vants another fencing partner." With that he rose and walked slowly from the mess hall.

Uhura watched him go and then turned to Palmer and commented, "I'm going to have to talk to that boy. Soon."

Before Chekov could manage to make his way through the mess hall door, Dr. McCoy walked in, and Chekov had to pause to let the senior officer by.

"Ah," said the doctor, "Mr. Chekov. Well, Ensign, did you survive the ordeal?"

Chekov sighed inwardly. "Yes, Doctor. I still have my job."

McCoy smiled at the comment. "I see. Learn much in the process?"

A variety of answers formed in Chekov's mind, ranging from amusing to acerbic, but the one he felt most comfortable saying aloud was "Quite a bit."

"Drop by to chat, if you feel like it," McCoy said. "Soon. A healthy mind and all that."

Chekov nodded and excused himself, seeking safety from well-meaning people. He had not walked more than ten yards from the room when he was nearly knocked down by Sulu, attired in a bright teal blue running suit.

After apologizing, the helmsman straightened up and said, "I was looking for you, Pavel. Come on, we're both off shift now. After I finish this run, I'm going to get Angela Martine into the botany lab to help me. We could use an extra hand."

"Just vhere do you get all this energy?" Chekov asked.

"Chocolate. The chocolate gives me the pep, and the exercise keeps me trim. Elegant solution, don't you think?"

"I suppose. Actually, Sulu, I vas going to my cabin while I can still be alone. I . . . I guess I still have some things to think about."

Sulu eyed his friend closely and nodded. "Okay, but don't get mired in too deep. If you do, call and I'll drag you out into the real world." Smiling again, he turned and resumed his jog, finally disappearing around a bend in the corridor.

Chekov headed straight for the turbolift and waited a few seconds while the computers routed a compartment to his position. When the doors opened, there stood Scotty, his arms full of data padds. Chekov suppressed a chuckle, seeing the chief engineer in such a situation.

"Don't laugh, laddie. Damnedest thing I ever saw. Five yeomen get the same glitch in their padds at the same time. Ye can imagine the trouble that might cause," Scott said with exasperation in his voice.

"I suppose so," Chekov replied, entering. "Deck six."

"What's troublin' ye, Ensign? Things turned out pretty well for ye, didn't they?"

Chekov turned toward Scott and managed a smile. "I suppose so."

"You said that already. Well, while I have you, I do want to thank you for your help in our investigations. Keep it up and you'll be a senior officer in no time."

"Thank you, Mr. Scott." Then Chekov lapsed into silence. Scott was perceptive enough to take the hint.

Within seconds the lift deposited Chekov on his own deck. With a measured gait he headed for his cabin. At last, a refuge from well-meaning officers and friends! Sure, they were only trying to cheer him up—and he had done well, finally.

But Chekov knew that if he had goofed seriously once, he could do so again. As far as the captain was concerned, he no doubt still had a lot of proving to do.

He had not been to his cabin in a while, and the sight of the repair crews working on the torn metal bulkheads surprised him. The ship had really been severely damaged in spots. What was more, a number of crewmen had died; there had been an announcement earlier about memorial services. Such a waste, he thought, rounding a corner—and was so wrapped up in his thoughts that he didn't see the approaching figure of Spock until it was too late to avoid a collision.

"I'm sorry, Mr. Spock," Chekov said, feeling a flush color his cheeks.

"No trouble, Ensign." Spock placed his hands behind his back, signaling Chekov that they were about to have a discussion, not a casual chat. "Actually, I am glad I ran into you. Your performance during the last few days has given me ample opportunity to monitor your skills. I find that you are more than a competent navigator."

Chekov was surprised. Coming from Spock, that was high praise.

"Nonetheless . . ."

The Russian frowned. Why did there have to be a "nonetheless"?

". . . you also display proficiency at the science station," the Vulcan finished. "I would like to know if you have considered exploring opportunities within my department."

Chekov went numb with disbelief. Not just a compliment, but an invitation to join the science section? What next?

"I, ah, well, Mr. Spock, I had not thought about it. And I certainly do like filling in for you. Yes, sir, I would like that opportunity."

"Indeed," Spock replied. The two men paused a moment as Spock considered the new information. "If I may ask, what are your ultimate ambitions within Starfleet?"

"Command," Chekov said evenly, finally putting into spoken words his heartfelt desire since he'd entered the Academy. "I want to work my way up through the ranks."

"A logical approach, Ensign. I shall keep this in mind as we evaluate duty rosters and assignments. Your skills at more than one station will certainly be taken into consideration. Thank you for your time."

Understanding that the conversation was over, Chekov nodded and waited for Spock to move away before continuing back to his quarters. This was certainly turning into the longest simple walk in his career.

Chekov picked up his pace and hurried to his room before he ran into someone else wishing to cheer him up. Everyone meant well, he realized, but it was becoming overwhelming.

Unfortunately the only one whose praise really counted was Captain Kirk. After his outburst on the bridge during a battle situation, would the captain ever have confidence in his abilities again?

Chekov was scheduled for the landing party at Gamma II, their next port of call. Would Kirk trust him with something even as basic as studying an automated astrogation station?

Finally reaching his cabin door, the Russian sighed with relief. The door opened instantly; at the same time, the automatic lighting system brought illumination up to a normal setting. Chekov plopped himself down on his bunk, hand behind his head, and just let his mind drift.

He found the quiet of the room and the near-silent thrum of the ship engines comforting. They told him things were back to normal. There were no more threats from the Rithramen raiders or the Parath'aa. And especially no plasma cannon, a device he had been seriously happy to see Sulu blow up. The universe did not need any more engines of destruction.

Just as he was about to drift off into some needed sleep, Chekov was disturbed by the door buzzer. Cursing to himself, he invited the visitor in. He'd expected Sulu or Uhura—but was caught off-guard when he saw the figure of Captain Kirk framed in the doorway.

Quickly the ensign scrambled to his feet, tugging at his shirt, wondering how messy his hair was.

Kirk held up a hand and gestured for Chekov to sit. To his credit, the captain also took a seat in front of the ensign's desk. The captain surveyed the room for a moment, allowing Chekov a chance to regroup his wits.

"The double rooms were smaller when I was on the *Farragut,*" Kirk said quietly. "My first roommate and I had to compromise on every decoration. I placed a hologram of my family over the dresser, and his girl friend's picture stood right next to it. People thought she dated both of us."

Chekov wasn't sure how to respond—or even if he should. Kirk was obviously making an effort to *talk* to him, not lecture, and he had to see how this was going to go. Chekov did make sure he sat up and paid attention. After all, this was the first time he'd ever heard the captain reminisce about his previous assignments.

Kirk went on. "It wasn't that long ago I was an eager ensign, sure I knew something from my Academy studies that the old man in the center seat might not have known. The difference was, Mr. Chekov, that I knew when to keep my theories to myself.

"I want the best from my people, and I will ask for opinions when time permits. You know our briefing room meetings are always open forums for discussion. But—and here's where you let me down—when I'm on the bridge, I don't want any discussion. A surfeit of options can be a distraction from the matter at hand. Sometimes those few seconds are critical—look what happened with the plasma cannon. Ten seconds between charges. That's precious little time for a debate."

Chekov nodded glumly and was waiting to hear his impending demotion to auxiliary control.

"You've served me well in the months you've been aboard this vessel," Kirk continued. "Your navigational skills are quite good, and I like seeing the way you and Sulu work together. Our planetside experiences have certainly proved you a capable field officer. So tell me, what should I do with you?" The captain looked steadily at the younger man.

Chekov pondered the question, looking up briefly at his commanding officer. He felt so young in Kirk's presence, though the difference was less a matter of age than of experience.

Was that what it took to become a legend? Battle-hardened experience? Was that all he was missing? Chekov wondered. Or would he never be the captain that Kirk was?

Abruptly he remembered that Kirk was waiting for a response.

"I expect some form of discipline" was all he could think of to say. "I am not proud of vhat I did on the bridge during our first encounter vith the raiders."

His voice was flat, monotone. He lowered his eyes and waited for Kirk's reaction.

"I have been watching you, Ensign. So have your friends. You've been beating yourself up pretty good since your mistake. I can't think of a better punishment than that." The captain paused. "You know, I see something of myself in you, and that may have clouded my judgment. I may have ridden you harder at Alpha Xaridian than I needed to. That may have caused you to overreact on the bridge. But I also like to think that the experience contributed to your excellent performance since that incident."

Kirk stood, walked over to Chekov, and held out his hand. "You have the potential for a fine career in Starfleet," he said. "I know this ship could use you."

The ensign couldn't believe his ears. He couldn't believe that Kirk was letting him off so easily.

But wait, he was punishing himself again, wasn't he? He had to stop that—the captain had said so.

Silently Chekov stood and gripped Kirk's hand.

The two officers shook, and Kirk gave Chekov his best smile—the one alien leaders bent under, the one that had a legendary effect on beautiful women. It was just one of the many weapons in the captain's arsenal.

"Thank you, sir. You may treat me in whatever fashion you choose . . . just as long as I can retain your respect."

"Acknowledged, Ensign. Now, with that said and done, it's time I reported to the bridge." Kirk turned to leave and then stopped in the opening doorway. He looked back over his shoulder, a grin on his face. "Oh, and good luck with Yeoman Landon."

Chekov blanched. Were there no secrets at all on this ship?

Kirk excused himself, chuckling at the astonished expression on Chekov's face. Things had been far too grim for far too long, he noted, as he walked back to the turbolift.

The captain was satisfied that Chekov would be around for a long time on the *Enterprise,* plotting course after course. It was only fair that he'd returned the favor by plotting a course for Chekov—one that would ultimately enable him to achieve his goals.

In the meantime there was a capable young officer at the navigation controls. And for today, that was enough.

THE EXPLOSIVE NEW

STAR TREK®

HARDCOVER

PROBE

by
Margaret Wander Bonanno

Pocket Books is proud to present PROBE, an epic length novel that continues the story of the movie STAR TREK IV.

PROBE reveals the secrets behind the mysterious probe that almost destroyed Earth—and whose reappearance now sends Captain Kirk, Mr. Spock, and their shipmates hurtling into unparalleled danger…and unsurpassed discovery.

The Romulan Praetor is dead, and with his passing, the Empire he ruled is in chaos. Now on a small planet in the heart of the Neutral Zone, representatives of the United Federation of Planets and the Empire have gathered to discuss initiating an era of true peace. But the talks are disrupted by a sudden defection—and as accusations of betrayal and treachery swirl around the conference table, news of the probe's reappearance in Romulan space arrives. And the *Enterprise* crew find themselves headed for a final confrontation with not only the probe—but the Romulan Empire.

Available In Hardcover
from Pocket Books

POCKET
BOOKS

106-03

REUNION

Michael Jan Friedman

Captain Picard's
past and present
collide on board the
USS *Enterprise*™

POCKET
B O O K S